THE POTION
AND OTHER PERILOUS LIBATIONS

BY

MATIAS TRAVIESO-DIAZ

Praise For
Matias Travieso-Diaz

"No matter how bizarre, strange, or twisted the story, Travieso-Diaz's living, breathing characters are the life's blood of the tale... there's more than enough wonder and dread for any fan of horror or dark fantasy."
~ Jason J. McCuiston, author of *Project Notebook* and The Last Star Warden series

"[Matias Travieso-Diaz's] stories remind readers the world can be a very scary place indeed."
~ Adrian Ludens, author of *The Tension of a Coming Storm* and *Bottled Spirits & Other Dark Tales*

"Mr. Travieso-Diaz's short stories are like the bloody news photograph you know you should not look at, but click on anyway... [he] leads you to the realization that terror begins in the familiar places, the hearth, the school, and the office, metastasizes into the terrors that haunt us collectively, and transforms banal, complacent souls into monsters."
~ Alex Ferraté

"The imagination that Matias brings to us through his stories is a treasure worth savoring."
~ Paul Gaukler

"The author has tucked a burr in our souls and left us itching and squirming. And that is as it should be."
~ Stephen Kimmerling

Also From
Dark Owl Publishing

Collections

The Dark Walk Forward
Baby Monster
John S. McFarland

The Last Star Warden:
Volumes I and II
The Phantom World
The Crimson Star Saga
    Episodes
Jason J. McCuiston

The Brotherhood of Secret
    Darkness and Other Cults,
    Cabals, and Conspiracies
Professor Wyrd's World of
    Wonders: Miracles and
    Monsters
Jason J. McCuiston

The Satchel and Other
    Terrors
Matias Travieso-Diaz

Tales from New Pangea
Kevin M. Folliard

No Lesser Angels, No Greater
    Devils
Laura J. Campbell

The Tension of a Coming
    Storm
Adrian Ludens

The Nightmare Cycle
Lawrence Dagstine

The Art of Ghost Writing
Alistair Rey

Bad Dreams and Reflections
Trevor Kennedy

Welcome to Scar Ridge
Jonathon Mast

Of Dark Places
Gustavo Bondoni

Vanther the Vanquisher:
    Bloodquest
Scott Harper

Anthologies
Something Wicked This Way
    Rides

Novels
The Black Garden
The Mother of Centuries,
  the sequel to *The Black*
  Garden
John S. McFarland

The Keeper of Tales
Jonathon Mast

Carnivore Keepers
Kevin M. Folliard

The Wicked Twisted Road
D.S. Hamilton

For Young Readers
Annette: A Big, Hairy Mom
Annette: A Big, Hairy
  Grandma
John S. McFarland

Shivers, Scares, and
  Goosebumps
Shivers, Scares, and Chills
Vonnie Winslow Crist

Buy the books for Kindle and in paperback
www.darkowlpublishing.com

TABLE OF CONTENTS

THE POTION

Holy song of thanksgiving of a Convalescent to the Deity, in the Lydian Mode
- Title of the Third Movement of Beethoven's String Quartet No. 15, Op. 132

I felt the end was near. After years of struggling against physical and emotional adversity, my body was finally giving up the fight. A malevolent intruder grew in my stomach, bringing a deep discomfort and pain that sapped my energy and forced me from time to time to stop all forms of activity, including—alas—composing.

This final malady could not have come at a worse time. I had been busy working on my Fifth Symphony, into which I was pouring a lifetime of learning and experience; I expected it would be my most important work. When the stomach pain struck, I had finished the Allegro first movement and was bringing the Minuet close to completion. The progress of the infirmity distracted me to the point that I could barely hold a quill in my trembling hand. I would stop writing and turn my attention inward, to examine the progress of the disease and lament the destruction it was leaving in its wake.

Doctor after doctor saw me, prescribing a wide range of treatments – elixirs, emetics, bleedings, hot- and cold-water treatments. I submitted to all, but none seemed to have any effect save make my disposition more and more sullen.

A couple of physicians suggested that spending a few weeks in the countryside, eating simple foods and breathing air free of contaminants, would help cleanse my body of pernicious humors. I consented to the suggestion because I have always loved nature and the idea of a retreat from civilization was increasingly appealing. So, in the early summer, I moved to lodgings in a small village in the mountains, many leagues away from the hubbub of the city. Physicians were scarce in those parts, and while the quality of the treatment arguably diminished, what I lost in patent draughts was gained in peace of mind.

One afternoon I was dozing off, forgetting for a moment my pain, when I was awakened by the arrival of an unexpected visitor who made himself known to the inn's owner as "Doctor Mirabilis, come all the way from Illyria." When asked to state the nature of his business, the visitor indicated, "It has come to my attention that a famous man has taken residence in this establishment, and I have certain business to transact with him."

This overheard exchange left me fully awake and seething with anger, for I had sought refuge in the country partly to escape the idlers and well-wishers whose importuning had made my debilitated condition worse. I put on my slippers and walked out into the common room, ready to castigate the interloper for invading my privacy. My plans were thwarted when the visitor moved briskly in my direction and extended a bony hand that eagerly seized mine.

"My dear sir, I feel so privileged by the opportunity of meeting you!"

I was startled for a moment by the effusive greeting and, before I could collect myself and reprimand the visitor, the man continued:

"Dr. Schildhorn, who I believe has been your physician for a number of years, mentioned that you were in ill health and informed me of your general whereabouts, and I made haste to come and offer my services to you!"

Schildhorn was one of the arguably best qualified among the charlatans who had attempted to cure my gastric malady. I made a note, however, to dismiss him as one of my doctors and maybe take some future action to punish his indiscretion.

At the moment, I replied coolly, "How do you know Dr. Schildhorn?"

"I used to practice medicine for a while in Basel, and at the time he was an intern at the University Hospital. We became friendly and have kept in touch over the years."

"How did he come to mention my name?"

"In my recent visit to Vienna, I had dinner with him, and he bragged a little about the famous people from all over the Empire he has treated. Naturally, your name came up at once and he alluded to your current indisposition."

"And what is your specialty?"

At this, the man was silent for a second and I had an opportunity to take a closer look at him. He had a swarthy complexion and was quite tall and thin. His face was dominated by a large, aquiline nose, and his massive head appeared even larger by the tangled mess of black curly hair that crowned it. More than a sober physician, he resembled a carnival performer of sorts.

"In general," he finally replied, "I fix seriously broken things."

"What do you mean?"

"For present purposes," he continued, "suffice it to say that I have developed a medicinal draught that cures most physical afflictions. I have come to offer it to you."

My negative feelings towards Doctor Mirabilis were enhanced by the obvious quackery he was attempting to foist on me. "Are you a fool, sir, or are you taking me for one?"

Doctor Mirabilis smiled deprecatingly. "It is not important whether I am foolish or not. What matters is whether what I offer can alleviate your suffering."

"That, I doubt very much. Good day." I turned my back, heading towards my room.

"Would you at least consider giving my medication a little trial?"

"What do you mean?"

He produced a silver flask from a coat pocket. I noticed, for the first time, that he was wearing heavy winter clothes though the summer weather was balmy. There was definitely something odd about the man.

"Please humor me by trying a sample of my potion in a glass of water, and judge the results for yourself." He went to a sideboard, picked up a pitcher and a wine glass, and filled the glass with water. He then lifted the stopper from his flask and carefully poured a few drops into the wine glass. The water immediately became turbid and acquired a greenish hue. "Here, try this" he offered.

"I will do nothing of the sort," I replied indignantly. "How do I know you are not trying to poison me?"

"Well, I'll show you." he drank a couple of gulps from the glass.

Nothing happened.

Doctor Mirabilis set the wine glass on the table and stared at me. "Well, are you going to try it?"

I scowled but, recognizing that the challenge was hard to evade, picked up the glass and brought it to my lips and drank a mere sip. The taste was bitter but bracing.

A strange mix of sensations then overtook me. On the one hand, I felt dullness, befuddlement, as if waking up in a strange room, unable to find my moorings. At the same time, the intense pain in my stomach seemed to have abated and become a distant discomfort.

"What is happening?" I asked in confusion.

"It is a foretaste of the future," replied the doctor. "This elixir will subdue the pain and, if taken in sufficient quantity over some period of time, will eradicate the disease that afflicts you. Drink it regularly for two or three weeks and you will be cured."

"That seems too good to be true," I protested.

Doctor Mirabilis coughed and issued a short, awkward laugh. "Well, there is a little something... a small physical price that you would have to pay."

"What is the price?" I bristled. The thought of the popular tragedy of Doctor Faust immediately came to mind. Was

I being offered a bargain that would damn my immortal soul?

"Nothing to worry about," replied Doctor Mirabilis, waving his hands as if dismissing my reluctance. "This medicine works in part by dulling sensations, including pain. Drink it and the sharp feelings and emotions that you might otherwise experience will be erased. You will feel calm and free from the ups and downs that bedevil most people. You will experience peace, perhaps for the first time in your life."

I let the implications of these words sink in, as the temporary relief from the sample began to fade and mental sharpness and physical pain returned. "Would I be able to compose once I achieved that blissful state?" I retorted.

"I can't opine as to that," replied Doctor Mirabilis. "I'm not a composer and my exposure to music is limited to what I hear in the taverns. I suppose that some types of music with more emotional content would be harder to write after taking this medication."

Alarm bells were already ringing in my head when I asked the next question. "Would there be a way to experiment? I mean, drink a little and stop to see what it does?"

For the first time in our meeting my visitor showed signs of disquiet. "I don't think so. In order for the treatment to be effective, the medication must be allowed to run its course completely. If the treatment is only partial, you may not get cured, but the dullness side effect may nonetheless persist."

"I see. One more question: How much will this treatment cost me?"

"We can discuss the fee later. However, it won't be much. It will be a great honor for me to restore the health of such an illustrious man."

"And perhaps you will let the world know of your great deed?"

The man's skin was too dark to register a full blush, but I noticed something in his expression akin to embarrassment. "I suppose I may," he acknowledged.

"I need to think about this," I concluded. "Please come back in a couple of days and I will let you know my feelings on the matter."

"As you wish," replied Doctor Mirabilis. "I will give my address to the landlady. Please summon me when you are ready to discuss treatment details. In the meantime, should I leave the flask with you in case you want to sample the potion's properties again? It is almost empty."

I was about to turn down the offer, but a sharp pang of pain from my midriff made me change my mind. "Thanks." I replied curtly, pocketing the flask. "Have a good day."

* * *

I began wrestling with the problem the moment the door of the inn closed behind Doctor Mirabilis. I was highly suspicious of the doctor. The man was definitely some sort of scoundrel, but was not demanding payment, so outright fraud was probably out of the picture. On the other hand, he had a lot to gain—in prestige and perhaps in the ability to peddle his invention—if he could point to me as a satisfied customer.

Given his interest in making the sale, I expected he would probably play down the negative side effects of administering the potion, including the decline of my mental faculties. Thus, I had to assume that should I pursue the treatment I would become a dullard and my musical career would come to an end.

If the medicine worked as intended, on the other hand, I would be cured and I might embark on a decade or more in which to enjoy life and perhaps move into a new phase as conductor, pianist, or music teacher.

Which was more important? My life or my art? I suspect that the answer might be different depending on when it was posed. And there lay the rub, for at this moment I was in the midst of writing a masterpiece that could well be the crowning point of my career. Should I prolong my life at the risk of being unable to finish the symphony? Yet, the suffering caused by the malady was leaving me paralyzed and almost unable to continue writing. What to do?

I spent a couple of sleepless nights agonizing over the dilemma. On the third day, I wrote a short note and had it delivered to Doctor Mirabilis. In essence it said thanks for your offer, but I must decline it. I will continue to fight this battle on my own.

* * *

My greatest personal strength is the ability to write music that reflects the conflicts in my soul, my efforts to master adversity, my views of the world and my fellow men. I decided to draw on that strength to help me overcome my physical weaknesses. I would remain in the country, would take such medications as appeared beneficial, would eat sparingly and as healthily as I could. And I would force myself to continue composing, no matter what the pain.

I discovered that, for me, composing was an effective short-term medication. There is strength in music making that helps one transcend the foibles of the body. My health continued to fail, but my soul burned bright through the creative process.

I wrote the Adagio, the third movement of the symphony, between the summer and fall of that year. Like my physical condition, the music oscillates between passages of immense pain and others of joyful resolve to prevail; it ends having all the pain and the joyfulness merge in a contemplative counterpoint. Writing the last movement, an impassioned Allegro, went quickly on the heels of the Adagio.

I premiered the symphony in November to acclaim by the critics and the public. Perhaps the Adagio will be played at my funeral, when that day comes.

* * *

Late in December, around Christmas, I sat by the fire, not thinking of much, just enjoying the warmth and cheer of this, my last holiday season. The flames drew fantastic shapes, some of which reminded me of creatures from the stories grandma would tell me in my early years. I felt at peace and ready to take leave of the world.

The pressure of a hand on my shoulder brought me back to reality. With some difficulty, I turned my head and focused my sight on the man standing by the armchair. Recognition was accompanied by an unpleasant jolt. It was Doctor Schildhorn, who I had stopped seeing after my meeting with Mirabilis last summer. I still resented Schildhorn's indiscretion, which had nearly caused me to give up my career in the hope of better health. I scowled and greeted him harshly.

"What are you doing here, Schildhorn? Didn't I leave instructions with my housekeeper not to let anyone disturb me?"

"Don't blame Mathilde. I told her that I had some urgent news to impart and she let me in, since she has known me for years."

"And what is the important news that gives you leave to bother me?"

Schildhorn lowered his head. "There is no news. I know you no longer employ me as your doctor, and I have just become aware of the reason for my falling out of favor. I have come to offer my apologies. This being the holiday season I am hoping you will find it in your heart to forgive me."

I looked at him reproachfully, so he went on. "I hardly know the man who calls himself Doctor Mirabilis; we were mere tavern acquaintances in Basel, and I know nothing about his medical skills, if any. By plying me with wine, he was able to extract from me information that allowed him to locate you. This was a gross error on my part, and I am truly sorry for it."

I still did not reply, so he followed up with a question. "What did he say to you? Was he trying to sell you something?"

I broke down and summarized in a few words my conversation with Mirabilis. Schildhorn took a deep breath and commented, "You were wise in turning down his offer to supply you with his potion. I expect that it was some addictive drug that would have left you in thrall to him. After a while he would have started demanding money to continue the 'treatment' and you might not have been able to refuse."

My response appeared to surprise Schildhorn. "I actually tried what was left in the flask he left with me. The stuff seems to work; my pain was gone for a couple of days. At the end, however, my refusal was grounded more on a weighing of my priorities than on any reservations about Mirabilis's character. See, were he to appear before me now, when my most important work is done, I might take him up on his offer."

"But would you really give up your mind and perhaps your freedom to add more months to your life?"

"Possibly. That is a difficult question. Life is precious, and anything that prolongs it is worth considering. I have managed to continue composing even though my remaining days are few. I no longer write symphonies, but simpler things like piano sonatas and songs. As long as I breathe and my mind is active, I can get new things done. Perhaps that is the secret of a life well lived; do as many useful things as you can, big or small, in the time that Fate has granted you. Yet, were he to come back and offer me that flask, I might take him up on it. But I have had no need to resolve the issue because Mirabilis has not come before me again."

Schildhorn then surprised me. With a broad smile that barely concealed his duplicity, he confessed, "Actually, I know Doctor Mirabilis rather well now. I spoke to him recently and he asked me to beg you to give him another chance to provide you with his elixir. Would you consider meeting with him?"

I was appalled by Schildborn's chicanery, yet my response was quick. "I am willing to meet with Mirabilis again, but I am unsure of the outcome. I will see what he has to offer."

"So, for you whether to prolong life is still not a simple question," wondered Schildhorn.

"Life and death decisions never are," I responded.

LAST SUPPER

And now, the end is near
And so I face that final curtain
My friend, I'll say it clear
I'll state my case, of which I'm certain
I've lived a life that's full
I traveled each and every highway
And more, much more than this
I did it my way
- Paul Anka, Claude Francois, Jacques Revaux,
and Gilles Thibault

1

It was all over. After years of motions, pleas, trials, and appeals, Antonio Quiroga's emergency application for a stay of execution was denied by the U.S. Supreme Court and his death sentence by lethal injection was scheduled to be carried out at the Central Prison in Raleigh. The execution was set for seven a.m. on Monday, October 21.

Antonio and his pro-bono, ACLU-appointed lawyer had steadfastly maintained his innocence and argued that ethnic, anti-immigration bias was behind his conviction. It was uncontested that Antonio had shot a police officer responding to a call of a break-in at a liquor store. The alleged circumstances under which the shooting took place, however, were particularly gruesome: it was said that the officer, a white female, had been disarmed and was begging for her life as Antonio taunted her with her own pistol before shooting her in the temple.

The sole eyewitness to the homicide was Matthew Cartwright, the liquor store owner, who had been preparing to close the shop when Antonio came in, "obviously intoxicated." Cartwright testified that Antonio had been raucous and disorderly and had demanded to be given the contents of the cash register. Cartwright had pressed a button under the counter that triggered an alarm at a nearby police station; the alarm had been installed after several attempts at holding up the store, which was in a low-income section of Raleigh.

According to Cartwright, when the female officer arrived, Antonio—who was over six feet tall and more than two hundred pounds heavy—jumped on her, overpowered her, wrestled her gun away, and taunted and then executed her.

Antonio, testifying in his own defense, asserted that the officer had been abusive and had "pistol whipped" him; and that they had fought and the gun had accidentally gone off, killing her. Forensic analyses found fingerprints from both Antonio and the officer on the gun.

At the first trial, the presiding judge had refused to admit into evidence as "speculative" several pieces of potential testimony to the effect that Cartwright was a notorious right-wing extremist with links to the American Nazi Party and the KKK. The only testimony regarding Cartwright's character came from a Southern Baptist minister and a Rotary Club member, both of whom testified that Cartwright was a man of high integrity and outstanding moral character.

The all-white jury in the first trial convicted Antonio of first-degree murder with aggravating circumstances, which resulted in the judge issuing a death sentence against the defendant. The judgment had been overturned on appeal, based on the judge's failure to admit potentially impeaching testimony against Cartwright.

The second trial had been similar to the first, except that the impeaching testimony against Cartwright was admitted, as well as additional laudatory testimony by two of Cartwright's neighbors and a gun shop owner. Another all-white jury had deliberated for only an hour before convicting Antonio.

2

When Antonio was advised by Harry, his pro-bono lawyer, of the failure of their last appeal, he was angry but expressed no surprise. "A Mexican can't get no justice in this country," he said. "When are they going to do this?"

"Two days from now, first thing Monday morning."

"And how are they going to do it?"

"By lethal injection. They'll give you a shot of sodium thiopental as tranquilizer, combined with a couple of drugs that will kill you."

"Will it be painful?"

"We argued that the thiopental is an ultrashort-acting anesthetic that may wear off and lead you to regain consciousness, such that you could actually be awake and experience great pain and distress as you died. If that were the case, you wouldn't be able to express your pain, because you would have been rendered paralyzed by a paralytic agent. The Supreme Court rejected this argument as conjectural. The truth is that we don't know what will happen, other than that you will be dead in a matter of minutes."

"Those bastards! They kill you and don't even give a damn how much you suffer!" There was a long pause. "Can I demand they finish me off some other way?"

"No. Death by injection has been approved by the Supreme Court."

Another, very long pause. "Will they give me a nice last meal?"

"They will. Usually, the State will let a death row inmate

choose his last meal as long as the choice is reasonable. Often the meal includes steak, some alcoholic beverage, and ice cream or pie. Do you have any preference in mind?"

"I've got to think on this. I'll tell you tomorrow morning."

3

"Have you decided what you want for your last meal?"

Antonio answered Harry with an unexpected question. "Is there any real good seafood restaurant here in Raleigh?"

"I hear the seafood at a French restaurant called Chez Michel is very good. I've never been there, because it's pricey and I can't afford it."

"Could you pull up their online menu on your laptop?"

"Sure."

They looked together at the menu for a few minutes and Antonio announced his choice.

"This is what I want: First, peanut soup 'a la Senegalese,' whatever that means. Then, this scallop appetizer, I don't know how to pronounce it."

"Coquilles St Jacques," offered Harry.

"That. And for the main course, 'Lobster Thermidor.'"

"Thermidor. You're going all seafood! Anything else?"

"Maybe some wine. What do you recommend?"

"For a seafood meal, you should get a bottle of white Loire wine. Here, they have a nice Sancerre. It's sixty dollars a bottle, but you're not paying for it."

"Can you put an order for me, to be delivered here at the prison about eight p.m. on Sunday?"

"I'll have to get approval from the Warden, since he'll be footing the bill."

"Well, go do it. That's what I'm *not* paying you for." The smile on Antonio's face surprised the lawyer.

4

Harry had trouble getting the State to provide Antonio with the last meal of his choice. Eric Wagstaff, the Central Prison Warden, was incredulous when Antonio's lawyer handed him a written request with the inmate's choices and the selected source of the dishes. "French food? French wine? What does a wetback know of French food? How about some fajitas, or tacos, or maybe a burrito?"

"Sir, with all due respect, that is the most racist thing I've heard from a North Carolina public official in the last ten years. Do you mean to tell me that because my client is a Latino he is not entitled to have his last wishes satisfied?"

"Look, this meal is going to set us back a couple hundred dollars. This guy is not going to even properly digest it before we pull the plug on him. It's a waste of money, and I'm not going to do it."

"Sir, please reconsider. Think of it as a kindness, an act of generosity towards a condemned man who you are going to put to death right afterwards."

"No way! I don't want to do it and won't! Bring me a decent request or your client will have to go to his death on an empty stomach!"

Harry decided it was time to play hardball. "I guess I'll have to tell the *Raleigh News* of your decision. I'm sure it will make the Sunday front page. And CNN has been covering my client's case for years. They will probably have something to say about your sending a poor immigrant to his death on an empty stomach. Should I tell the *Times*, too?"

Wagstaff blanched. He was new to his position as Warden and did not relish getting involved in a civil rights controversy. "You wouldn't dare!" he threatened.

Harry pulled out his cell phone and looked up a number. He dialed. When a female voice responded, he inquired: "Yes, can I speak with Albert Crawley at the City Desk? This is Harry Hudson calling."

Wagstaff ran his index finger across his neck, motioning Harry to abort the call. Harry complied.

"All right, I'll let him have his French dinner. But only on condition that you keep this thing quiet. I don't want every death row inmate to start demanding a fancy sendoff."

"You got it," replied Harry.

5

Harry placed the order himself, describing the situation to the maître d' and suggesting, somewhat disingenuously, that this unique request could result in a lot of free publicity for Chez Michel. Accordingly, the restaurant applied special care in preparing the order and having it delivered in foam insulated bags to keep it appropriately hot. The guards at the Central Prison had been alerted to the delivery and took custody of the two bags of food and a cold shipping box containing the wine. They brought it all to Antonio's cell and placed the contents on the built-in table against the back wall. The restaurant had provided plastic utensils and drinkware, as well as linen napkins to accompany the meal.

The two guards uncorked the bottle of wine and stationed themselves outside the cell, ready to watch the proceedings. Harry shushed them away: "Please have some decency. Let the man enjoy his last supper in privacy." Reluctantly, they stepped out.

6

The peanut soup was tasty and quite nourishing. It was silky and smooth, spicy without overwhelming the palate. It was full of the taste of its main ingredient, without a cloying reminder of peanut butter. Antonio reflected that, under normal circumstances, a bowl of soup like this and some bread, like the slices from the baguette that came with it, would have been enough to satisfy him. He ate every delicious spoonful, poured himself a glass of Sancerre and marveled at the clean, bracing taste of the wine, full of exotic flavors: lime, grapefruit, green apple, pear, honeydew melon. He had never tasted anything like this before. It was so deliciously complex!

But he must eat. He opened a Styrofoam box containing his appetizer, the Coquilles St. Jacques. He had tasted scallops only once in his life and he had not enjoyed the experience, thus he approached the dish with some trepidation. He needed not have worried. The box was brimming with delicate scallops, shrimp, and mushrooms swimming in a rich cheese and white wine sauce topped with breadcrumbs. It was golden and still bubbling a little when he put a fork on it. He devoured it all and drank the sauce for good measure. Another glass of Sancerre helped him down the splendid appetizer.

He felt sated, but knew he had to complete eating his meal. Opening the largest of the Styrofoam boxes, he did a double take as his eyes rested on the spectacle of the succulent chunks of lobster meat that had been cooked in a rich sauce, a creamy mixture of egg yolks and brandy, stuffed back into a lobster shell, and browned with a Gruyère cheese crust. A small mound of saffron rice accompanied the dish.

To Antonio's unsophisticated palate, accustomed to an entirely different sort of cuisine, this outlandish dish was too much, particularly after the scallops appetizer. But he soldiered on: one delicious bite after another, washed down with the dwindling supply of Sancerre. As he forced down his last morsel, he started feeling fatigue and wished he had ordered some black coffee.

Seconds later, sharp tingling started on Antonio's tongue, mouth and throat. The tingling became a swelling, and his throat constricted. He broke into convulsions and fell to the floor of the cell, breathing laboriously.

7

When the guards returned to Antonio's cell, they found the prisoner on the floor, unconscious, vomiting through swollen lips. "Quick, get some help!" shouted one of the guards. A couple of minutes later, a medic came to the cell, looked at Antonio, who was barely breathing, and declared, "He may be having a heart attack." He called for a stretcher.

As they were lifting Antonio's inert body, the medic saw the remains of the dinner on the table in the back of the room. "Did he just have dinner?"

"Yes, a few minutes ago," replied the guard.

"What did he have?"

The guard seemed puzzled by the question. "Why, he made a big deal of what he wanted and got himself a lobster and a fancy plate of scallops, and Cajun peanut soup…"

"That's it!" replied the medic. "He had an allergic reaction to what he ate. We'll have to give him an epinephrine shot right away."

"Does he need to be taken to the infirmary?"

"Absolutely. We'll need to put a tube down his mouth or do a tracheostomy. I just hope we are not too late. He seems to be in bad shape."

Just as they were wheeling him away, Antonio started quieting down and his breathing seemed to be slowly returning to normal. The medic motioned the attendants to stop.

"Is he coming out of it?" wondered the guard.

"Sometimes allergic reactions, even bad ones, run their course quickly. We still will want to empty his stomach and give him some steroids or antihistamines to bring his system back into balance."

Antonio opened his eyes and moaned. "Where am I?"

The guard replied with a sneer. "Right where you were. Your last supper didn't seem to agree with you."

"Oh" came back Antonio, clearly disappointed. "So, it didn't work. Am I still going to be executed tomorrow?"

"Actually, no. Given your condition, the execution would have to be postponed. In any case, the Governor showed his yellow streak. He just issued a stay of your execution pending further reviews of the evidence."

"How come he did that?"

"The election is in ten days and the death penalty, specifically your death, has become a campaign issue. The polls are running in favor of abolishing the death penalty, so he punted and is playing for time."

"Do I get to stay in this rat hole?"

"Until you are executed or you croak by yourself, as you almost did a moment ago."

"That's terrible."

"What's the matter, don't you like it over here?"

Antonio's reply was lost as the gurney carrying him turned a corner and disappeared from view.

As they went into the infirmary, Harry asked his client, "Did you know you are allergic to seafood?"

"Of course, to both shellfish *and* peanuts. I was going for the daily double."

Antonio then asked his lawyer in earnest, "Listen, Harry, now you got more time to figure how to save me. I was unwilling to let those bastards cause me more pain by taking my life with that injection. But I still want to live, so please give it another try, will ya?"

"I'll see what I can do, but I can't promise anything. I made all the arguments that I could already."

"So, they'll kill me no matter what?"

"Possibly. The powers that be have the cards stacked against you."

"Well, I better start thinking of the menu for another last dinner. Would you please find me a Japanese restaurant that will cook blowfish?"

The Taste of Blood

*Blood is really warm, it's like drinking hot chocolate
but with more screaming.*
- Ryan Mecum

The process through which I arrived at my current condition was agonizingly slow, taking year after year of accumulating practices and manias. After the death of my parents in my mid-twenties, I left the small town where I had grown and moved to this big city. In doing so, my life started to go on autopilot; I took, and promptly gave up, a position in an accounting firm and drifted from there to a meaningless manual job and then to another, just enough to keep me going. Alone in the city, I shed my few out of town friends and relations little by little without caring or even noticing the loss.

Over time I developed a routine. At the end of every work day, I would leave the shop or warehouse where I was then employed and pick up some fast food to take home. I would bring the dinner to my barren apartment and would eat it slowly, masking its blandness with catsup and drowning it with cheap beer, while I watched the local and national news and the early evening game shows. After dinner, I would go online and surf through the social sites, never participating but taking in the ceaseless flow of political commentary, religious homilies, war reports, news of family events, and bits of celebrity gossip. I would play a couple of rounds of video games (the gorier the better), at the end of which I would turn to the prime-time TV shows. If a football or basketball game was being broadcast, I would watch it while smoking a couple of cigarettes and would drink more beer. Sometimes I would watch a porn movie and pleasure myself before falling asleep; outside those electronic carnal events, I only had marginal dealings with members of the fair sex.

On weekends, my routine varied somewhat from that on workdays. During the week I had to get out of the apartment to do whatever was necessary to earn a paycheck, whereas on Saturdays and Sundays I would, weather permitting, leave the apartment for a solitary walk in my favorite park, a short distance away from my apartment complex. There, I would sit on a bench by a small pond and stare vacantly at the birds hunting for morsels under the waters and the turtles in their ponderous transit along the muddy banks. Children would ride by me on their bikes, joggers would pant back and forth on the path a few inches from my bench, walkers would stride by, chatting to each other, and sometimes would drop a greeting at me. I hardly noticed the human traffic and paid no attention to it.

Days, weeks, months, seasons went by like this without leaving a trace. I lost track of time, but I guess five or six years went by monotonously since I arrived at the city.

Without realizing it, I proceeded to throttle all human emotions and isolated myself from the outside world during that time. I shed many mental functions, leaving only those of the reptilian "old brain" where the most primitive instincts reside: hunger, sex drive, self-preservation. I began to steadily lose my humanity.

***

The few people with whom I interacted were those that suffered from similar emotional handicaps to mine, people who were lacking in enthusiasm or strong interests, and were content to deal with me at a superficial level. Such people never challenged me or disagreed with my actions or opinions, such as they were. I would go out drinking or take part in innocuous activities with them, like playing pool or poker or watching a game on TV, without ever engaging in any meaningful conversations. Virtually all the people in this category were co-workers who had drifted through life until they reached conditions not unlike mine.

One of my occasional companions was a man five years younger than I named Zeke. We worked together at a carpentry shop, cutting, shaping, and fastening together pieces of wood and plastic to construct furniture and other items for the home. Zeke was a more experienced woodworker than I and more than once he helped me put together a fancy chair or side table in accordance with a customer's requirements. Neither of us thought much about the help Zeke was rendering me, but our frequent contacts led to a relationship as close to friendship as either of us was capable of sustaining. Zeke would come to my apartment every once in a while to watch an important game, and I would likewise pay infrequent visits to the modest home Zeke and his sister had inherited from dead relatives.

Zeke's sister, several years younger than he, was as different from him as two members of the same family can ever be. Elaine, or "Leni" as everyone called her, was outspoken, vocal, and kind hearted. She was also pretty in an unassuming, straightforward sort of way that did not threaten other girls or bring out the lascivious side of her male acquaintances. She was perfectly suited for her job as an elementary school teacher, though she would have also done well as a nurse or a retirement home caretaker.

My dormant sexual urges were instantly awakened when I met Leni. Even though she did nothing to arouse a man's base passions, her positive persona drew my attention and activated one of the alert elements in my reptilian brain, the urge to find a mate and copulate. It was perhaps the total difference in our personalities that attracted me to her.

I was not so far gone from the normal world as to act clumsily on my cravings and impose on her, but started dealing with the girl in a manner akin to a courtship. I began visiting Zeke more frequently, sometimes on the flimsiest of excuses. For those visits, I would dress a little better, and would make an effort to appear well groomed. I had figured out Leni's schedule—she was out on Tuesday and Thursday evenings, to attend meetings of charitable organizations of which she was a member—but was otherwise at home most other nights. I scheduled these visits to Zeke to avoid the days she was absent.

When we met, I tried to make pleasant conversation with Leni and feigned interest in the social issues to which she referred frequently: care for the homeless, child welfare, drug rehabilitation. She was always passionate about those matters, and I could not figure out whether she saw through my clumsy attempts at appearing responsive to her concerns. In any event, her extroverted personality dominated our conversations and saved me from needing to be too expressive.

After a while, I felt I was making progress in getting somewhere with Leni, as our talks got more personal and intimate. Perhaps I was gaining ground in her estimation; however, that progress was to be ultimately negated by the events that were to transpire between us.

Being open and inquisitive, Leni began probing into my habits, my behavior, my isolation, my lack of any strong beliefs: the kinds of topics whose frank discussion, for normal people, would have fostered greater intimacy. But I didn't like to be cross-examined on the details of my life or confronted with the oddness of my behavior. I felt under attack, and the primitive portion of my brain reacted with resentment and developed an increasing need to fight back on her intrusions. I throttled my resentment for fear that, if expressed, it would be detrimental or even fatal to our relationship.

Matters came to a head one Monday night, when I invited myself to Zeke's house to watch a professional football game. At halftime, Leni and I went out to the porch holding our drinks. After a couple of desultory exchanges about the game, she turned to me and said in a serious tone, "Todd, I need to tell you something. I am worried about you. I sense you are leading a rudderless life, drifting from one meaningless thing to another without purpose or plan. I like you, but you need to take stock of yourself and start acting like a regular human being before our friendship can get any closer. I can help you, if you wish."

I felt a shock of pain and surprise, as if I had been bitten by a rattlesnake. I sat silently for a few moments, feeling my face drain of color. The long-repressed anger then started rising in my chest, and I was shouting when I replied, pounding on the arms of the chair. "What business is that of yours? What right do you have to criticize me or find fault with my lifestyle? Do I ever berate you for your silly charity projects? Do me a favor and shut the hell up!"

Leni seemed surprised and, at first, did not react to my outburst. Finally, her school teacher training kicked in. She got up, livid but silent, and left the porch without saying a word. She did not speak to me again the rest of my visit to her house.

It would have been much better if we had traded insults in a shouting match that allowed me to let off all the accumulated steam; that way I could have just written Leni off as a romantic prospect, become indifferent to her, and forgotten that she even existed. Faced with her silence, I sullenly left the house a few minutes later, telling Zeke that the game was too boring to watch, and returned to my apartment to stew in unrelieved anger over the way Leni had abused me.

* * *

My mood did not get better as the week went by. I probably knew in my heart that Leni's criticisms were valid, but could not bring myself to acknowledge that the life I led was a total waste, so I blamed and resented Leni for raising cruel and unjust accusations against me. By the weekend my unvented anger at her had reached the boiling point.

Four of the carpentry shop employees would get together some Saturday nights to play pool at a tavern close to work.

That Saturday I was not in the mood for joining the others in a game, so I called Zeke and complained that I had a mounting headache and intended to stay home and go to bed early. That was indeed my plan but, as I tossed and turned in bed, I realized that I was too upset to sleep and needed some fresh air. I got dressed and went out to walk randomly into the night.

My stroll took me to the vicinity of Zeke's house and the obsession that festered in my mind coalesced into a decision: I would see Leni and demand a retraction.

I knocked on her door several times before the girl called out: "Who is it?"

"It's me, Todd," I grunted.

"Zeke is not here," she replied in a tone that made it clear she did not wish to talk to me.

"That's fine," I replied. "I need to speak with you."

There was a moment's hesitation, and then Leni answered. "It's late, Todd. I was already in bed. Can it wait until tomorrow?"

I replied in a quivering voice, "No, it's rather urgent."

There was an audible sigh and the door swung open.

We stood in silence in the entryway, staring at each other; then she asked, "What was it that you wanted us to talk about? Is it about your rude outburst the other night?" Apparently, Leni was expecting *me* to say *I* was sorry for screaming at her, for she crossed her arms, in the unyielding pose she would probably take before a wayward student. Keeping my temper barely under control, I stood with his fists tightly closed and replied, very slowly but in a threating tone, "Actually, I want *you* to apologize for the nasty things you said about me."

Leni gasped. "Are you serious? You should look into mending your ways rather than demanding apologies from me."

I was seething with indignation and no longer able to respond with words. I burst into the living room, lunged at Leni, seized her shoulders, and shook her violently. "Apologize, I said!" I cried.

"No, I won't. Let me go and get out!"

We struggled, Leni trying to free herself and my hands moving from her shoulders to her neck, choking her. Our gyrations led us back to the front door, against which I pressed her body. Leni pummeled my chest, but I ignored her blows and tightened my hold on her throat. I was far stronger than the girl and began drawing all the air out of her lungs.

Leni started to slide towards the floor and blindly reached out for support. Her hand touched a stand next to the door and landed on her umbrella, which she seized and used as an improvised weapon, hitting me repeatedly on the arms and neck, trying to force a release of the mortal hold on her neck.

The umbrella was a flimsy bit of pink fabric and aluminum, and the blows she delivered with it served only to further enrage me. I stopped trying to choke her and began pounding her head against the door, striking over and over as she cried and writhed in agony. Finally, she stopped fighting and went limp.

I dragged her inert body to the living room and stretched her on the floor. Blood was streaming from the back of her head, turning her blond hair into a sticky mess. Her breath was coming out as irregular gasps, and after a while it ceased.

I regarded the girl's prone figure with confusion. I felt some regret over what I had done; however, the most intense emotion I experienced was elation. I had finally silenced the bitch, punished her lack of respect.

I was still panting from the effort and felt that my throat was parched and sore; perhaps I had screamed as I fought with Leni without realizing it. I felt a sudden thirst, and the immediate need to quench it. I bent over Leni's body and started to lick the blood that was now streaming out of her broken skull.

My first taste of human blood was unsettling. It was salty and had a metallic undertone; drinking it, I sensed, was a gross, repulsive act. Yet, I kept savoring the blood and otherwise venting my fury on the cadaver until I realized I must leave the house quickly, before Zeke returned.

***

Back at home, I played back in my mind all that had occurred since I decided to take that stroll. I still felt no guilt, but was filled with growing satisfaction. My contentment only turned to fear when a new thought occurred to me: I must have left multiple fingerprints and DNA samples at the site of the murder, and soon the police would be coming to arrest me for the crime. I had to get away.

I filled a backpack with as many valuables and essentials as I could carry and left the apartment. Stopping at an ATM, I emptied my bank account and walked in the direction of my favorite park, to sit and consider my next steps.

The place had an eerie feel in the middle of the night, bereft of human and most animal life; its solitude felt unthreatening to me and was comforting. I sat on my bench by the pond and reflected on my uncertain future. In the morning, I might try to hitch a ride out of the city and move away, somewhere in the countryside, perhaps to a faraway village where I could resume the monotonous existence to which I was accustomed.

Yet, the welcoming silence that surrounded me suggested something else. The big city was probably the best place for me to hide in plain sight. I would join the homeless people that dwelt anonymously under the bridges and expressway underpasses. With luck I could avoid capture, or at least delay it for a long time.

But in turning into a creature of the shadows, my needs and appetites evolved. I became a zombie, a monster that survived by preying on victims I selected and hunted, or those who by accident walked into one of my hideouts. I preferred young ones, violating their bodies, sampling their blood, and partaking of their still throbbing flesh with insane relish. The grotesque mutilations of the victims I left behind became cover page photographs in the more sensational publications. Other newspapers and magazines limited themselves to describing the terrible deeds I committed with sober words that only suggested to the reader that the hidden truths were even more terrifying. For although I was commonly described as a modern vampire, the desecrations I inflicted on my victims went beyond those that the likes of Bram Stoker would have imagined.

I became an urban legend, and media reports of my exploits stoked the city dwellers' fears during their waking hours and brought renewed terror when I appeared to haunt them in their nightmares.

The police hunted me relentlessly but, as their efforts to track me down mounted, my ability to hide and disguise myself also increased. Within a couple of months of starting my nighttime rounds I had developed an inventory of suitable places to hide, like the nearly inaccessible laundry room in a rundown apartment complex or a forgotten access to a sewer tunnel.

I was ultimately captured. I barely escaped death at the hands of the police, was tried and ruled to be insane, and was committed to an asylum, from where I am relating my story to a reporter from a popular tabloid.

I will never be released and may leave this world soon—there are many who wish me dead, some perhaps inside this prison. But by the time I was imprisoned I had already reached a personal success: my life was no longer rudderless but had achieved meaning. So, I will welcome death, in whatever time and manner it chooses to visit me.

Spring Flowers

Our memory is our coherence, our reason, our feeling,
even our action. Without it we are nothing.
- Luis Buñuel

It was April, time for planting annuals in front of Sam's house. This was something that he had never needed to undertake, for it was one of the many tasks his wife carried out single-handedly. Now she was gone, and it was another obligation he had been forced to assume while trying to cope with his staggering grief.

In front of the house were two large clay pots that were to be filled with flowers that would bloom continuously until frost, in late October or November. Those flowers added a splash of color that made Sam's house, a conventional brick colonial, more inviting to visitors and added to the home's curb appeal. He needed to take care of filling those pots as soon as possible, for he intended to put the house on the market in a matter of weeks and wanted it to look presentable. His ultimate plan was to move into an assisted living facility and leave as many of his memories as he could behind with the house.

Sam was planning to order these annuals from a catalog, since it would be too painful for him to go alone to one of the garden centers that he and Edith used to visit each spring looking for fresh flowers to purchase. He decided to fill the pots with the same annuals his wife planted every year, for they were heat and drought resistant and came in several colors, though they had always bought the intense scarlet variety that contrasted well with the brick of the house walls. His wife had liked these plants because they grew low, spread out throughout the pot nicely, and could be noticed from the street; best of all, they seldom required watering or any other care. He agreed with her assessment and decided to get them.

Now, what were they called? They had owned these plants for years, but at this time he seemed unable to recall their names. *No problem*, he told himself. *I'll flip through the catalog, and I'll find them.* He opened a printed nursery catalog he kept for reference and, to his surprise, found nothing that resembled the plants he used to see adorning his driveway year in and year out. He went online and searched through articles on annual flowers, seed catalogs, garden supply sites, and other botanical sources. Nothing: the plants were not depicted anywhere in any of the references he consulted. It was as if they never existed.

But he was sure they did exist. For one thing, he had seen those plants in yards all over the country, and hanging from balconies everywhere in Europe, like in Italy, Germany, Austria, the Netherlands. He went through the European pictures in his digital image collection and found nothing like the blooms he had seen during his vacations. Petunias, yes. Pansies, impatiens, begonias, irises, roses, yes. The mysterious plants he had thought he remembered so well were conspicuously absent.

He went to sleep, mystified. After a restless night, he woke up, still thinking of the beloved flowers that apparently had disappeared from the face of the earth. And then, trying to get his arms around the mystery, he made a discovery: he could not remember any more what the plants he had kept in the pots by the entrance of his home looked like, so he would be unable to rely on his recollection to find them by sight.

* * *

He tried to reconstruct the last day's search for the flowering plants and focused again on his European vacations. He seemed to recall there was one country in which the plants he sought were often found, displayed on balconies, stone urns, doorways, any place where flower pots could be placed, for the country's warm and dry weather was favorable to the plants. It was a small country next to Italy, with a coastline right on the Adriatic Sea. What was its name?

Sam realized he had no idea, and started to panic. Forgetting a plant was one thing; losing track of an entire country where he and his wife had spent joyful days was something else. He rushed to the world globe he had kept since high school. Sure enough, the Italian boot was there, immediately recognizable. However, across the Adriatic there was a large indentation he did not recall seeing before. Opposite Italy, the Adriatic extended a long distance to the east, touching on Slovenia, Hungary, Bosnia and Serbia. How could that be? Was his mind playing tricks on him?

Not only that. After a while, Sam could no longer remember ever having been to a place on the Adriatic teeming with the flowering houseplants he sought. In that extended vacation in which he and his wife drove through Austria and then south into the Balkans, he could remember Maribor and Szeged and Belgrade, but was not aware of having gone into another country west of Serbia, assuming there was one.

***

Sam then recalled that they had met another American couple at their hotel in Vienna and enjoyed their company so much that he and Edith had decided to modify their vacation itinerary; they would give up on their planned trip east to Budapest and Warsaw and instead travel south with the other couple into the Balkans, which they did and had a great time. After their return to America, the two couples had kept in touch by phone and email—the others lived somewhere in the West Coast, he and Edith in the Atlantic seaboard—and exchanged Christmas and birthday cards, reporting on the events of their lives. Those people had become good friends and surely would remember where they all had gone on their joint vacation.

What was the fellow's name? Sam did not seem to remember, but expected he would find him on the directory of friends and family that was saved in his laptop.

He went through every entry in the directory three times, and could not find a listing for either the husband or the wife of the couple. *This is ridiculous*, Sam told himself, exasperated. He went through all his saved emails on two different servers and could not find any messages to or from the elusive couple. Worse yet, after three hours of searching, he came to realize he no longer knew who he was searching for or why. And he became really scared.

* * *

As in several recent occasions, Sam could not consult his wife on this question, for she had been dead for several months. Her family—or his—would probably be incapable of filling in the specific gaps in his recollection, and bringing the problem to their attention would only cause them to become concerned about his afflicted state of mind as a widower or his mental health. He decided to confide in his best friend Janos, who knew as much about Sam's comings and goings over the years as any person alive. He placed a mid-afternoon call to Janos.

"Buddy, I need to talk to you urgently. Can you have a beer with me as soon as possible?"

"I can come in a couple of hours, right after work. Is that soon enough?"

"Yes. Let's meet at the usual place. I'm buying."

"See you then."

* * *

He greeted Janos and they sat at their favorite spot, away from the bar. Sam was too jittery for beer, so before starting his conversation with Janos he had a quick scotch, neat. And then another. And still another. He had just ordered the fourth one when Janos squeezed his shoulder. "Come on, Sam. Get hold of yourself. You haven't told me yet what's going on, and we have been here for almost half an hour. What seems to be the problem?"

Sam sighed and opened up. "I think I am losing my mind. I'm trying to sell my house to get away from all the memories of my life with Edith. And, do you remember how we always keep two large clay pots on the driveway of our home, a few steps from the front door?"

"I guess so, but..."

"Well, we always put new flowering plants in those pots this time of the year, and I wanted to do the same thing to get the house ready to be listed. Yesterday, I couldn't recall what plants we placed on those pots, and the ones that for a moment I thought we had used don't show up anywhere I've looked."

"That's odd but shouldn't be the cause for alarm, I think. You must be confusing the plants you want with some others that don't exist. Go buy something else!"

"Well, it gets better. I seemed to recall seeing those plants everywhere in one country in the Balkans, on the last trip Edith and I took to Europe seven years ago. Do you remember that trip?"

"Sure, you brought us a nice set of cut crystal goblets from Prague."

"Well, I can't find the country where I thought I had seen those plants. It doesn't show up on any maps or articles on the Balkans."

"Now, *that's* impossible. Where was that country that you can no longer find?"

"It sits directly across from Italy and has an extended coast on the Adriatic. It has some nice coastal cities, and borders Bosnia and Serbia, and Hungary as well."

"My friend, I have not been to that part of Europe, so I can't be sure whether such a place exists."

The fourth glass of scotch was then delivered. Sam downed it in three gulps, placed a fifty-dollar bill on the table, and ran away without saying goodbye.

* * *

Sam woke up in the early morning bearing all the signs of a punishing hangover. His stomach ached as if he had eaten coals, he had trouble keeping his eyes focused, and a terrible headache was mounting by the moment. What had he done the night before to cause all this discomfort?

He must have been drinking. Alone? He never got drunk at home, a practice he still maintained out of respect for Edith, even after her death. He must have gone out with one of his friends. His fuzzy mind started focusing. Yes, he had been at a lounge with someone, but who?

A trickle of ice coursed through his veins as he tried to focus on the previous night's events, and then a thought came to him. Yes, he had been drinking with a friend, a very close one whom he had known for many years, but he could not pinpoint his name or conjure up his appearance.

Sam dragged himself to the bathroom, and threw up interminably, trying to remove the alcohol from his system and clear his mind. Doing this made things a little better, so he walked into the kitchen and poured himself a glass of tomato juice, a popular cure for hangovers. He despised tomato juice and only drank it as a last resort.

He sat at the kitchen counter, dutifully downing one gulp after another of the revolting liquid. As he did so, Sam ran through his mind the names and faces of all his friends, close and casual, even acquaintances. One by one, they were considered and rejected. "That's not him... not him ... not her, either..." As each person was brought up and discarded, he or she disappeared from his consciousness, and did not return when he tried to go down the list again.

And the horrible truth finally revealed itself. He was running out of memories. He just had to think of something or somebody and an image of the subject would flash before his eyes, and then, after a while, it would vanish. Every memory that his brain had accumulated over seventy-odd years of existence was fleeing, leaving his mind as empty as the house where he now lived.

He ran to his laptop. He experienced a moment of relief when he verified that his business records were still intact, and so were miscellaneous files containing movies, songs, books from his collection. Then his search hit a snag. He had a directory containing all his photographic records – both the images of the pictures of his family and friends, which he had accumulated over a lifetime, and more mundane pictures of places he had visited and other images he had collected from various sources. He had spent many an hour over the years converting slides into digital images and scanning old photographs so he could show them on the laptop or in a separate picture viewer that he kept on his desk. The directory was half empty: the mundane pictures of animals, places, aquatic life, and so on were still there. Yet, the files that contained pictures of his friends and family were gone.

Then, a second pass through the directory containing all his images showed that it had become empty.

He did not dare look at the other directories containing copies of all the things he collected because he was certain that, by now, all these records would be gone, too. So, he was not only losing the memories lodged in his brain but also the physical evidence that the subjects of his memories ever existed.

"*No, no, no!*" Sam cried to himself. "*Edith, please help me!*" Invoking his dead wife immediately brought before his eyes the image of a still beautiful woman, her face contorted by recent disease and pain. In a moment, the image flickered and disappeared, leaving Sam with a feeling of unbearable emptiness.

Sam returned to the bathroom and, after looking through the unfamiliar shelves, retrieved a nearly full bottle of what, according to the label, were sleeping pills that someone must have kept to fight insomnia. Little by little, he downed all the pills, washing them down with gulps of water.

He had forgotten why he had gone to the bathroom, but shuffled semiconsciously to the bedroom and laid down. He wondered who he was and why he felt so tired. His eyes closed the moment his head hit the pillow.

* * *

The knocks on his front door became louder and more insistent. "Sam, open up! I know you are there! I need to talk to you!" After a while, the banging ceased, and much later was replaced by the sounds of a key turning on a lock and the door opening.

"Thank you, Emilia. I was about to call the police when Sam didn't answer my calls or open the door when I pounded on it, and then I remembered he had once given me your number as a replacement for my cleaning lady, who had gone back to Bolivia…"

They approached the bedroom. Sam was sprawled on his bed, spittle dripping out of his open mouth. He was breathing with difficulty and kept whispering incoherent words every few seconds.

As they tried to revive him, Sam uttered an anguished cry. "A wife! Did I have a wife?"

And then there was silence.

ORANGE

In dim eclipse, disastrous twilight sheds on half the nations,
and with fear of change perplexes monarchs.
- John Milton

The Mayan K'iche' people were engaged in a bitter war against their neighbors the Kaqchikels. The K'iche's launched a raid on Iximché, the capital of the Kaqchikels. The attack failed and resulted in many of K'iche's noblemen and warriors being killed. Those in the raiding party that survived were captured and confined to an underground prison in Iximché.

Four months after their capture, there were nine K'iche' captives left in the prison: Lord Jasaw, his first-born son Taavi, and seven noble warriors. One morning, a contingent of guards arrived and forced all captives to march across the city to a holding cell across from the Iximché main pyramid. It was sunny and cool, and the perspiration that covered the prisoners' bodies that morning was not caused by exertion, but fear.

"Why are they taking us to the temple?" asked Taavi.

"I'm not versed in the study of the heavens," replied his father, "but I seem to recall a prediction that sometime soon there will be a Chi'bal K'iin, an eating of the sun."

"What is that?" asked Taavi.

"It is a very dangerous time, for K'inich Ahau will disappear from the sky. He will travel in the underworld and may not re-emerge. I was about your age the last time this happened and I remember being scared out of my wits."

"What can people do to prevent the sun from being eaten?"

"Everybody bangs metal objects and people dance to the rhythm of the big drums, so that the noise helps wake up the sun."

Taavi persisted. "But what does all that have to do with us?"

Jasaw hesitated for a moment, and then replied, "Some primitive people believe that blood shed during human sacrifices will strengthen K'inich Ahau and help him fight the malignant forces that would keep him in the underworld."

Taavi asked yet another question. "Are the Kaqchikel people primitive?"

"Very," grunted his father.

* * *

When the prisoners arrived at the holding pen, soldiers removed their clothes, dabbed their bodies in blue paint, and placed headdresses of colorful feathers on their heads. One of the prisoners was dragged to the pyramid and taken to the altar at the summit. By the time he arrived at the altar, a sliver of darkness was moving into the sun's orange face.

The ruling Kaqchikel overlord, the Ahpo Sotz'il, stood on the terrace at the top of the pyramid, wearing the regalia of his office; next to him was the high priest, the *chilan*, who intoned a chant beseeching the sun to return to shine on the people. The *chilan* then directed guards to place the prisoner lying on his back upon the sacrificial altar. The execution priest, the *nacom*, then proceeded to puncture the chest, arms and penis of the sacrificial victim with an obsidian knife and gathered the blood in a shallow cup that, once full, was emptied onto the stone image of the sun by the altar.

Then, as the guards restrained the wildly resisting victim, the *nacom* cut through his abdomen and pierced open the diaphragm, accessing the still beating heart from underneath his ribs, and removed it by cutting it away from the ligaments that held it in place. The *nacom* handed the heart to the *chilan*, who smeared its blood upon the image of the deity. The heart was then burned and the smoke fanned towards the god's image. The cadaver of the sacrificial victim was dismembered, and morsels of his flesh were handed out to the people attending the sacrifice, who rubbed the flesh clean and consumed it raw.

The guards then returned to the holding pen to seize another sacrificial victim. By then the eclipse had advanced so that a quarter of the sun's face was plunged in darkness.

***

Three and a half hours elapsed from the time the first victim was taken out of the holding pen to the moment in which K'inich Ahau's face was totally seen again. Near the end, only two prisoners had been left in the pen: Jasaw and his son Taavi.

Guards unlocked the door of the pen and headed towards Jasaw. The man recoiled. He could see that the sun's face was almost free of shadow; soon the eclipse would end. But time had run out.

In a voice that crackled with dread, he begged, "Take Taavi first! He's young and his sacrifice will be more pleasing to K'inich Ahau!"

The tableau froze for a moment, as guards assimilated the plea of the K'iche' lord. The leader of the guards seized Jasaw by the neck and began drawing him away, but stopped short as another voice was heard.

"Take me! Spare my father, please!"

All motion stopped again. The guard flung Jasaw aside and turned towards the boy, who shook visibly. The guard's mouth broke into a smile, a mixture of contempt and admiration. "Yes, the God would appreciate the sacrifice of a valiant young man more than that of a cowardly old fool. Let's go!"

As the guards pulled Taavi away, Jasaw leaned back against the back wall of the prison, panting. A thought kept circling inside his head. *I can sire other children, but there is only one of me.* Every time the craven idea rose, he tried to dismiss it, but he ultimately failed, for the thought aptly described the state of his mind.

Not long afterward, the sound of a desperate scream filled the air above the pyramid; a faint echo, in which Jasaw recognized the voice of Taavi, reached the depth of the holding cell. Jasaw crawled to the entrance of the cell and sighed with relief, as a full sun blazed through the door.

* * *

"The eclipse is over," intoned the *chilan*. "The chants and sacrifices have been fruitful and rescued the sun from the underworld."

"K'inich Ahau is restored and displays his full glory before us," exclaimed the ruler reverently. "Let us pay homage to him with one more sacrifice. Bring out another prisoner!"

Jasaw never heard those words, but lived long enough to experience their consequences.

Cactus Trips

Sometimes maybe you need an experience. The experience can be a person or it can be a drug. The experience opens a door that was there all the time but you never saw it.
- Melvin Burgess, *Smack*

I met Rico when we sat next to each other during the Introduction to Philosophy course. I was a freshman and he was already a junior, but our educational paths converged three days a week at eight a.m., when we fought to stay awake against the droning voice of the instructor. Rico was very friendly, and the harrowing experience made us increasingly close.

I lived in a freshman dorm, while Rico—an exchange student from Mexico—was a member of Phi Gamma Zeta and lived in an upscale fraternity house set by the woods near the campus. In November, the Fizzis threw a rushing bash and Rico invited me to drop by, perhaps hoping that I would eventually become a pledge and move there with him. The event was on a Friday night, and since there was no school the following day, I planned to come in late and stay until the early morning.

When I arrived, the party was in full swing and I soon found myself drinking booze and talking to the fraternity brothers. Across the room I finally saw Rico, who effusively greeted me. We had one drink after another and then he said, "Let's go to my room. I've got something to show you."

We went upstairs to his room, which was in typical male student condition: clothes, books, CDs, and all sorts of trash, covered the floors, the guest chair, and the surface of the bed.

"Sorry about the mess," Rico apologized, and took out a foil-wrapped package from a nightstand drawer. It contained a dozen or so dried grey-green, soft, disc-shaped buttons, three inches wide.

"What are those?" I asked.

"Buttons from a cactus similar to peyote. I just got them from my contacts back home. The cactus is rare and only grows in the mountains."

"What do these things do?"

"They'll give you the best trip you'll ever experience. You'll feel happy and relaxed and get wonderful visions. Want to try them?"

"Do they have any side effects? I've never used drugs and don't know how they'll affect me."

"People often throw up after having them, but aside from that you'll feel fine. In fact, better than fine. They aren't addictive."

I hesitated, but I was bombed and had lost my inhibitions. *That's what one goes to college for*, I told myself, *to try new experiences*. "How do you eat them?"

"Tear a button in small pieces and eat them slowly. Be careful, they are bitter. You may want to wash them down with beer." He seized one button and proceeded to demonstrate, grimacing after taking the first bite.

I followed his example and ate my button, one small piece at a time. The taste was terrible and I felt like vomiting, but washed the morsels with beer and, after a while, had consumed them all.

"Now what?" I asked.

"Now we wait. The buttons need to be digested for the drug to take effect."

"What do we do in the meantime?"

"I don't know. Grab another beer from the mini fridge, sit back and start thinking pleasant thoughts. I'll do the same."

* * *

I experienced some dry heaving after eating the button, but it passed. After a while, though, the world before my eyes changed. The room began expanding and shifting, the trash and other objects flew around as if driven by an invisible wind, the nightstand lamp cast multi-colored lights and odd shadows. The ground shifted under my feet and the ceiling moved dangerously towards my head. Rico was now wearing only a T-shirt and briefs and was lying in bed, his body shrouded in a surreal glow. He was moaning loudly, as if in pain. I tried to offer assistance, but my tongue had entirely filled my mouth and refused to articulate words.

Then visions were joined by the odd sensation that I was floating outside of space and time, in total awareness of myself. I could feel my nerves touching each cell in my body. I thought I could order my nails to grow, the hair on my chest to curl and expand, my muscles to tense. I was totally in command of my body and could direct the operation of each of my organs. I expected I could cause my heart to stop beating, but recoiled at the thought. Instead, I experimentally forced the gums to pull away from my teeth exposing their roots, and made them go back in place. The feeling of complete control over my physical self was empowering.

I got up from my chair. I looked at the distorted figure of Rico, lying in bed, immersed in some dream of his own. Suddenly, I became inexplicably angry, blaming Rico for whatever the buttons he had provided were doing to me. I stumbled in his direction, walking slowly towards him, arms swinging right and left, knees and hips flexed, back bent forward. As I advanced, my mouth opened at an impossible angle, and I growled inhumanly. I felt my fingernails curve, becoming talons, and saw my body hair darkening and becoming thick and springy. I raised my rigid arms to strike the chest of my friend, but at the last moment some residue of common sense took hold and I merely struck the top of his head. I turned around and fled the room, but as I ran out, a sudden greediness drove me to pick up the foil package containing the rest of the cactus buttons. *For the next time*, I promised myself.

Luckily, nobody was awake, and I left the fraternity building unnoticed as the morning sun started to usher the new day.

* * *

I slept most of Saturday and was still recovering on Sunday. When Monday dawned, I was rigid with apprehension as I returned to school, dreading the encounter with Rico. Would he charge me with assault, demand that the school take action against me? I considered cutting classes, but decided that sooner or later I would have to face the music.

Rico was already at his desk when I arrived. He had a black eye and a bandage over his right eyebrow. I started to apologize but he cut me off.

"I know you took the buttons! But you might as well have. I was out of it until mid-afternoon and if someone had gone into my room, they would have found the package in plain sight and I would have gotten into trouble."

"I'll pay you for them," I offered.

"Never mind," he replied. "I already ordered some more."

A tense moment of silence followed, and then I bit the bullet, needing to test the extent of his recollection. "What's with your face?"

"It's the funniest thing," he replied. "I woke up in pain, with a swollen face and a cut on my forehead. I must have fallen off the bed, but I can't remember a thing. Did that happen before you left?"

My sigh of relief could have been heard across campus. "No, you were sleeping like a baby," I lied.

"How did the drug hit you?" he asked.

"It was the weirdest experience of my whole life," I replied in all honesty. "But it was great, all things considered."

"I'm glad. Should we get together again?" He smiled, and his expression showed he hoped for a positive response. So, I replied cheerfully.

"Sure. You name it."

"Maybe next weekend? There is another party at the house."

"That will work."

"It should be fun. But you bring your own buttons this time, you hear? I'll tidy up my room for you, I promise," he said, and winked.

***

The next Fizzis' party was less well attended than the one the week before—just over a dozen guys drinking screwdrivers and engaging in desultory conversation. Rico was waiting for me at the entrance and immediately put a drink in my hand. "This party is dead. Let's go upstairs now," he urged.

We trotted up to his room. He had disposed of the trash and put his books, binders, and other objects on his desk, and made the bed. The room smelled as if he had sprayed air freshener.

"You've done a good job cleaning," I praised.

"I wanted to make sure your experience would be enjoyable," he replied. "Did you bring your buttons?"

I took the foil package from my jacket and waved it at him silently.

"Did you try them again before today?"

"No, I didn't dare," I replied.

"Well, let's make up for lost time," he answered, eagerness in his voice. He opened the nightstand drawer and produced another foil package, similar to the one I was holding. He then walked over to the mini fridge, opened it, and took out a bottle of purplish liquid.

"What is that?" I wondered aloud.

"Pomegranate juice. It works better than beer to mask the bitterness of the buttons." He produced two plastic cups and filled them with juice. "To a really good time," he toasted.

I sat on the guest chair, a button in one hand and a cup of juice in the other. He sat cross-legged on the bed in an identical posture. We chewed our buttons and drank the juice.

Minutes passed in silence. I closed my eyes and plunged into an amorphous dream, and then the drug-induced visions started. I felt again the sense of oneness with every cell in my body and decided that this time I would not move from my chair but would let the trip unfold and carry me wherever it chose. Ineffable peace filled my soul, and I was one with the universe. I felt I had gained knowledge of hidden truths that now revealed themselves in breathtaking beauty. I was experiencing bliss.

I was brought back to reality by the feeling of being touched. I opened my eyes and there he was: Rico was bending over my chair, running his fingers over my chest. I shuddered, still in the middle of my trip, but increasingly aware of my surroundings.

"It's okay," whispered Rico, opening my shirt and starting to press his hand over one of my nipples.

"What are you doing?" I challenged, my speech warped by the drug.

"Don't you like it?" he replied, his own voice also slurred.

I shuddered. "Let go!" I tried to demand, but only an incoherent grunt came out.

Rico's hand moved down from my chest towards my stomach.

I don't know how I would have behaved in normal circumstances. Under the influence of the drug, I jumped to my feet, growling. As I did, all my nerves became active, directing urgent commands to every corner of my body. I pushed Rico back to the bed, where he lay for a moment. He then started to get up.

I am almost six-feet-two and weigh two hundred-plus pounds. Rico was probably five-feet-nine and at most a hundred and fifty pounds heavy. He would never have been able to force himself on me, but he seemed driven on by the drug. He mumbled something in a thick voice, and came towards me.

By this time my body was bent forward, my arms extended down. I was pounding the floor angrily and uttering animal sounds. My threatening attitude should have been enough to make Rico retreat in terror, but he was in the middle of a trip and perhaps felt invincible. He squared his shoulders as if ready for a fight.

I charged. I seized one of Rico's wrists, twisting it until something broke with a sickening crunch. He yelped and tried to free himself, but I held his body as I dug my teeth into his chest, biting it wildly. I then landed repeated blows on his head until he ceased moving.

I flung the inert body, limp like a rag doll, on top of the bed, pounded my chest in triumph, and sat back on the chair, panting with excitement.

* * *

Some time passed, and reason returned slowly as the trip receded. I realized what I had done and was stricken with horror. Other emotions followed: remorse, self-loathing, pity for the poor bastard that laid on the bed. However, these feelings were accompanied by an urge to repeat the drug experiment under less challenging circumstances.

But the most critical task was to avoid getting caught. Again, the fraternity house was quiet in the early morning hours. I dragged Rico's corpse out of the building and dropped it in the woods. I had been seen with Rico and expected to be questioned by the police, but hopefully they would not be able to prove anything.

I went back to my dorm, armed with two foil packages full of cactus buttons. *Did I actually change into something else?* I wondered. There was no clear answer.

I must try this again and see what happens. This stash will last me until at least spring break, I mused. *By then I may need to find a supplier.*

The Honey Cake

People living deeply have no fear of death.
- Anaïs Nin

Contrary to the popular images, I do not play chess with those whose souls I am about to retrieve, or allow myself to be delayed or distracted as I carry out my task. I am Death, and am all business.

I can, however, be summoned, but it takes a very powerful mage to accomplish this. It was one such summoning, by the great mage of Caliph Al-Mu'tadid, that led to the events I shall relate.

At first, I resisted the summoning, but the mage persisted until, to get rid of his demands, I materialized in Al-Mu'tadid's chamber, and learned the Caliph's unusual story.

* * *

Al-Mu'tadid had many beautiful wives and concubines he had gathered from all over his empire. He kept them under guard in a harem, protected from the eyes of the populace. But it came to pass that the mother of one of these ladies fell ill and the daughter pleaded with the Caliph to let her travel to the village where her mother resided. The Caliph was partial to this girl and, making an exception to his confinement rule, allowed her to go visit her mother and render such succor as she could.

During the travel, the girl became acquainted with one of the guards escorting her caravan, who was the Caliph's nephew. The trip was long and the occasions in which the two traded pleasantries evolved into increasingly passionate romantic encounters. By the time they arrived at the village where the girl's mother lay, the girl and the boy had become lovers.

* * *

The girl's mother died shortly after the caravan's arrival, but the lovers decided to conceal her passing from the Caliph so they could extend their dalliance as long as possible. They swore to each other that they would remain together the rest of their days, no matter what happened.

The Caliph grew suspicious of the long absence of his wife and sent out spies to investigate. When the Caliph learned of the treachery of two people who had been close to his heart, his anger knew no limits. He sent an army to capture his unfaithful wife and his treasonous nephew and had them brought before him in chains. At the palace, they were placed in separate, contiguous cells, in which they lingered pending the Caliph's decision on their fate. As they awaited, each would repeat loudly to the other the vow to remain united until the end.

* * *

Weeks passed. The Caliph became incensed at their defiance and had his wife brought to him from the dungeon for questioning.

His anger abated somewhat at the sight of his beautiful bride, now exhibiting signs of the rigors of imprisonment. Al-Mu'tadid felt a pang of love for the woman who lay prostrate before him.

"Renounce your guilty attraction to my nephew and I'll release you to spend the rest of your days in a retreat to lead a life of reflection and devotion to Allah," he offered.

The girl responded with a question. "What will happen to him?"

"I'll have him beheaded."

"In that case, I won't renounce our love. I'll perish with him, for we have promised never to part from each other."

"I can force you to go to a retreat," threatened the Caliph.

"Do that and I'll kill myself. Either set us both free, or slay us both."

"It shall be as you wish," replied the Caliph.

***

Al-Mu'tadid started losing sleep from trying to think of ways of making his revenge against the guilty pair most exemplary. He discarded the idea of beheading them, for their demise would come swiftly and be almost painless. At the end, he ordered that a sepulcher be erected on the side of a hill that he could watch from the balcony of his bedroom. The lovers would be confined there, to choke slowly beside each other, each sensing helplessly in the darkness the struggle of the other to find one final puff of breath, until their lives were stifled in anguish.

The Caliph then thought of a further refinement on his idea. Was there a way to make one of the guilty pair die by asphyxiation in the presence of the other, but allow the survivor to linger on, suffering the torment of their separation? It was then that he asked his mage to summon me.

***

I was quick to express to the Caliph my annoyance at being summoned. "What is so important that requires me to appear before you? By your leave, I must attend to many pressing matters. Right now, plague is running rampant all over your kingdom; scores are dying each day. I must see to them."

I started to fade away, but Al-Mu'tadid's outcry stopped me. "Wait! I want to discuss with you the deaths of my nephew and one of my wives, who have dishonored me and have been sentenced to die slowly, by suffocation."

I reappeared. "What do you want me to do about that?"

"Is there a way that one of them might survive for a period, so that the survivor may experience the agony of being separated from the other?"

I had never been asked such a question. After some pondering, I replied, "There is an ancient enchantment, developed by the High Priests of Egypt, for the creation of a special kind of honey cake that can postpone the ending of life if it is fed to a living person. I cannot detach the soul from the body of a person who has eaten one of those delicacies until the cake has been fully digested and all traces of it have left the body of the person. That can take many weeks, for as long as even a particle of the cake remains in the body, it will repel me."

"Where can I get such a cake?"

"Every pharaoh's tomb has an antechamber where items of food and drink were stored for the dead ruler to get nourishment while he traveled in the afterlife. The cakes keep forever, and can be found in one of those tombs."

There was a long pause while the Caliph consulted with his mage. At the end, he had another question. "If one of the prisoners eats such a honey cake, can he or she stay alive while the other dies?"

"Yes, for however long it takes for the cake to disappear from the consumer's body. Are you going to have somebody bring one of those cakes to the sepulcher and offer it to them?"

"Yes. It has to be you to offer the cake and get one of them to eat it."

"Why me?"

"Because they will believe whatever you tell them. Who ever heard of Death being dishonest?"

"But why would I do such a thing?"

"Because if you do this for me, my mage will lift the spell that holds the holy city of Luz against your power. Right now, those who reside there enjoy exceedingly long lives, and linger among the living way past when, by the natural order of things, they should have surrendered their souls to you. I'm sure you find that situation a bit frustrating."

"Why don't you send your nephew or your wife to Luz while the other dies?"

"Because Luz is a holy city, where only those who are pure of heart may live. They are sinners, so neither may enter Luz."

"I can do this much," I replied. "I can bring a cake to the sepulcher, tell them of its properties, and say that one of them has the opportunity to survive for some time. But I shall not recommend anything."

"What if they shared the cake?"

"For the magic of the cake to work, it must be eaten in its entirety by a single person. Sharing it would render it ineffective."

There was another long consultation between the Caliph and his mage, at the end of which the Caliph proffered a variation of his deal. "What if you offered to set free whoever ate the cake? Could you do that?"

"Yes, I could propose transporting the person who ate the cake to some place outside the prison. Perhaps that would lead one of them to agree."

"Well, why don't you give it a try? You can have access to Luz if just one of them eats the cake and lives while you take the other."

"The deal you propose is unsavory, but would be beneficial to me. I shall do it."

* * *

It took the Caliph's agents weeks to break into a royal tomb in Egypt, seize a few honey cakes, and bring them to their master. I was summoned and the Caliph handed me one of the cakes. "We'll bury them alive in the sepulcher at sunset tomorrow. Go see them."

I scowled but took a honey cake; its touch burned like acid.

The following evening, I entered the walls of the sepulcher and confronted the guilty pair, who were sobbing and embracing each other, saying their farewells to the world.

They were fearful when I materialized in front of them. It was very dark in the room and they could not see my features, but my spear emits a faint phosphorescence that showed the outline of my skeletal form.

"Who are you?" challenged the boy.

"Death. I am here to carry your souls away."

"We're ready," declared the girl with false courage.

"But before I take you, I would like to present you with an alternative."

They remained silent, awaiting my next words.

"I have with me a magic honey cake. If one of you eats it, he or she will avoid dying in this tomb."

"How can that be so?" asked the boy. "I'm sure they will come in a couple of days from now to confirm we are dead. Anyone who is still alive will be slain."

"If you eat this honey cake, I will transport you to a hidden kingdom in the Pamir Mountains, where the power of the Caliph does not reach."

"Can't we both go there?"

"No. I can save only the person who eats the cake."

"What if we share it?"

"That will not work. One of you must eat the entire cake for its magic to be effective."

"We're not interested," replied the boy. "We have pledged to be with each other forever. Anything that separates us won't do."

"Well, the decision is yours. I will leave the cake here. Think about it. I shall return in a few hours."

* * *

Later, I returned to the sepulcher from a battlefield, having nearly tired myself collecting the souls of fighters from both armies. War leaves me weary; I prefer taking the spirits of the living one by one, so I can savor the lingering fear, the purposeless despair, the remorse and self-recriminations of my victims.

As I approached the sealed chamber where the profane lovers had been confined, I expected one of three scenarios to have played itself out. Either the boy had seized the honey cake and consumed it, or the girl had somehow taken it away from him, or, perhaps more likely, they had shared it, despite my warnings.

The sight that welcomed me as I entered the chamber surprised me. The couple was reclining against the rough stone walls of the sepulcher. They held each other in a tight embrace, and appeared unconscious or in a trance. On the floor, where I had left it, was the magic honey cake, untouched.

I approached them silently and, when I was in front of them, noticed their labored breaths, as they gasped to get fresh air in their lungs. I am insensitive to temperature, so I could only guess that the chamber was stiflingly hot and running out of breathable air. Soon they would asphyxiate.

I struck the ground three times with the barbed iron spear I use to seize souls off the bodies of the deceased. The sound of iron pounding on stone was dull but effective. The boy opened his eyes with great difficulty; a few moments later, the girl also became conscious.

"Why wake us up? You'll soon have us," asked the boy reproachfully.

It was my turn to remonstrate. "Of that, I am sure. But I must satisfy my curiosity first. Why did one of you not eat the honey cake and be transported to the Pamir Mountains?"

"We each tried very hard to convince the other to eat the cake. Neither of us would do it," explained the girl.

"We'd never do anything that would separate us!" added the boy. The girl, raising her head a little, nodded.

"My charge was to take one of you today, not both. This is a great disappointment." I could not but notice that I was sounding petulant, contrary to my sober manner.

"Sorry to have disrupted your plans," was the boy's sardonic reply. "But you'll have to wait a few minutes and take us both."

"Death waits for nobody," I responded. "Right now, there are a thousand other places I have to be."

"Then, why don't you kill us and be done with it?"

"I harvest the souls of people. I do not slay them."

"That's your problem. Now, go and let us die in peace."

I would have directed my rage at the youth, but violence is not in my charter. But I was furious: my distasteful deal with the Caliph had unraveled, and I had already wasted a lot of time on this sordid affair. Plus, I felt something akin to pity for the couple.

I struck the front wall of the sepulcher with my spear and blasted a huge hole to the outside. Through the opening, I could see the panic-stricken soldiers the Caliph had posted to guard the tomb disperse in all directions. Fresh air bathed the sepulcher and revived the prisoners.

"Go away," I instructed the lovers. "Get as far from here as you can. I shall meet you again soon."

The boy helped the girl to her feet and led her out the hole. As they left, he had the nerve to cast a cautionary directive at me. "Make sure you come for both of us at the same time!"

THE GIFT FROM THE GODDESS

Each person's life is like a mandala —
a vast, limitless circle.
- Pema Chodron

All genies are extraordinary, but the one I encountered during my trip to Lachung not long ago was particularly unusual, compared to the ways those beings are often described.

I am a well-known travel photographer. If you read the National Geographic or Smithsonian magazines, you may run into one of my photographic essays covering an exotic destination. It was the search for such a story that drove me to Lachung, the most remote village in India, near the border with Tibet. I went to Lachung to cover the famous Chaar mask dance to be conducted during the Tibetan New Year at the local Buddhist temple.

I got to the Lachung Gompa, as the monastery is called, on a cold afternoon in mid-February. The monastery was unremarkable: a small, two-story building sporting metal dragon sculptures outside an upstairs porch from which one could get nice views of a nearby river and the entire Lachung Valley. I snapped a few pictures and made ready for the dance to take place that evening.

As I walked around the back of the building, my eyes were drawn to a dirt path that wound its way up a mountain a few feet away from the monastery. When I asked one of the monks where the path led, he diffidently replied.

"There used to be another monastery near the top of that mountain. It was destroyed in an earthquake centuries ago. Only a few ruins remain of the place, and nobody goes there because the souls of the monks who perished in the disaster are said to haunt it."

"I would like to look at the ruins and maybe snap a picture or two. Is it far?"

"An hour or so of brisk walking, but you must be careful. The trail is steep and uneven and there may be wild animals and possibly poisonous snakes along the way."

"Don't worry. I always carry my heavy walking stick with me. My only concern is that the climb may be a challenge for my old knees."

* * *

It took me almost two hours of painful trudging to get to the rock ledge on which the ruins of the ancient temple were located. Much of the original structure had disappeared, victim to the ravages of time; all that remained, for the most part obscured by centuries of overgrowth, were piles of broken and decaying timber.

Disappointed, I was making ready to undertake the challenging walk down to Lachung when I noticed that portions of what once had been a building wall were still standing, though covered with vines. A dark foreboding seemed to radiate from the isolated structure; it both repelled and drew me in. After a moment, I came closer, and as I did, heard a low hum coming out of the wall.

As I approached further, I realized that the sound was emanating from the back of the structure. It took considerable effort to skirt the debris and vegetation that covered the ground, but I was finally in front of the source of the noise: a large rectangular bronze box, attached to the wall with pegs of the same material. The box surfaces were covered with a green patina and exhibited numerous decay spots, but were largely intact. From within the box came an ululation, a lament that spoke of great distress.

I told myself there could be nothing alive inside that box. However, the mysterious sound piqued my curiosity. I drew out my multi-tool and, selecting a sharp blade, began scraping at the surface of the box in search of a hidden opening. I found nothing of the sort, but in pressing against the enclosure I activated a catch inside it, causing the right side of the box to shift outwards a couple of inches. That was enough for me to grab the bottom edge of what was obviously a door and force it wide open.

The back of the box was lined with a coarse material resembling jute. Embedded in the lining was a mandala, a large circular weaving that was attached to the four corners of the box. The weaving was made of the same material as the lining, but was dyed white and contained a labyrinthic array of crushed black stones. The rim of the mandala was filled with odd symbols made of the same black stones. At the center of the mandala sat a dull red gem the size of a goose egg.

The noise I was hearing was coming from that egg. I reached for it but, before I could make contact, a shock coursed through my body, and a thought—like an unarticulated voice—rang in my mind. "Do not touch me, mortal, or you shall perish!"

I jumped back a couple of feet, my body suddenly covered in cold sweat. I was seized by panic and started to run away when the same voice spoke in my mind again. "I am trapped in this maze by a *bhikkhu's* enchantment. He and the others of his accursed kind died or ran away when the earth moved and everything but my prison collapsed. I now command you to set me free!"

I felt a strong compulsion to obey, but fear of whatever was trapped in that circle stopped me. "Why should I free you?" I responded aloud. "The monks that built this monastery were holy men. You must be evil for them to have imprisoned you in this mandala."

The voice in my head became angry. "Why do you mortals always speak of good and evil? All beings must do what their nature calls them to do. The only evil occurs when you act contrary to your true self!"

"Perhaps," I replied, "but how do I know you won't harm me if I let you out?"

"I promise I will not harm you if you release me," countered the voice.

"Well, that promise is a start," I replied, playing for time as I considered the possibilities of escape. "But, again, why should I take chances freeing you? What is in it for me?"

I felt the entity's anger in my head. "You do not trust me. Well, then, if you release me, I promise I will not harm you *and* I will grant you a wish."

"Any wish?"

"Well, any wish within the bounds of my powers. I am not allowed to create or end life. Nor can I bend another's will to give effect to yours."

I thought of all the fables I had heard as a child and all the books and movies that mentioned bargains with genies and weighed them against my current needs. I was in my late sixties, unattached, reasonably famous, and enjoying a good income. I was, however, already suffering the pains and indignities of old age, though I knew of no illnesses that were bound to bring about my immediate demise. "Can you make me young again?" I asked.

"That pushes against the limits of my powers but is not entirely prohibited," answered the genie's voice doubtfully. "I cannot do what you request myself, but would be able to take you to someone who might grant your wish."

"Who is that?"

"Lakshmi, the Hindu goddess of power and beauty. I serve her."

"Where do we find your mistress?"

"Lakshmi can be found everywhere, but her presence is most strongly felt in the temples dedicated to her, like the one in Kolhapur, south and west of here."

"And you would take me to her temple?"

"I would, and would bring you back here at the end of your appearance before her."

"And she would be able to restore my youth?"

"She could, but whether she would be willing to do so is up to her."

"Speak the truth, genie! What risks are there for me if I set you free and you take me before Lakshmi?"

"Your only risk is that the goddess may deny your request."

"That is a risk that I am willing to assume. We have a bargain. How do I go about setting you free?"

"My imprisonment is ordained in the words of a *mantra* inscribed on the rim of the mandala. Just remove one of the symbols in the *mantra* and the spell will be broken and I will be free again!"

I approached the mandala and broke off with my knife the stones that composed one of the symbols on its rim. As the black pebbles tumbled to the ground, the entire box started to shake and the red gem disengaged itself from the mandala and flew up into the sky, where it grew and changed shape until it became a transparent column of smoke and fire, towering above me and the monastery ruins. The column had at its top a terrifying simulacrum of a human face, with grotesquely elongated features, a hole where a nose should have been, fiery eyes, and a wide, scowling mouth.

I threw myself to the ground, instinctively looking for shelter. In my head, the genie mocked my reaction. "I have given my word not to harm you, so I cannot hurt you. But, blowing in the wind, I can fly us to Lakshmi's temple. Are you ready to go?"

"Yes," I gulped, and was lifted off the ground by an invisible force.

***

I have no recollection of whether I flew for minutes or hours, and only became conscious when my feet touched the ground in an esplanade facing a sprawling temple fronted by a hall with a conical spire. It was near sunset but the entrance to the temple was teeming with worshippers waiting for the opportunity of having a *darshan*, a visitation with the image of the goddess. Again, the genie whisked me inside the temple and through various rooms until I was standing before a bejeweled three-foot image of the goddess. Her black face was adorned with pearls and seemed to be gazing intently at the setting sun through an opening on the west wall.

I must have been invisible to the crowd that gathered around the statue but not to the goddess, whose exchange with the genie I could hear clearly. "Why are you here, my son, and who is this mortal that accompanies you?"

The genie's voice had a touch of unctuousness as it addressed the spirit within the icon. "Beloved Mother, I was held captive in a mandala by meddlesome Buddhists until this man freed me. I promised that I would bring him to seek a boon from you."

"What does he want? Money or power?"

"No, beloved Mother. This man is approaching the end of his time and wants to regain the freshness of youth and, if possible, extend his term on this sphere." The expansive wording of my request came as a surprise to me, and was perhaps a way for the genie to signify gratitude to me for his deliverance.

"I will not lengthen his life, for he has done nothing to warrant remaining among the living beyond his allotted time. I can, however, restore beauty to his countenance and impart new vigor to his body, but does he really want that this be done?"

For the first time, I dared to address the goddess. Lowering my head, I answered, "Reverend Mother, I do. I wish to gain renewed energy to better meet the demands of my work and my daily life."

I detected a small frown in the dark features of the icon. "You speak of the demands of your work. Do you realize that if I restore your body to that of a youth, your skills and experiences will also be reset to those of an immature, inexperienced young man?"

There was an awkward pause, while I digested the implications of Lakshmi's words. If I accepted her gift, I would lose all the life lessons I had acquired over so many years and become as ignorant and naïve as young people tend to be. Was I prepared to make such a trade?

I weighed my choices. The freshness and vitality of youth were alluring, particularly in my current physical condition. Yet, I had lived long, loved and suffered much, and learned a great deal. Was I willing to give all that up in exchange for increased wellbeing?

After thinking about it for a while, I concluded that the answer was no.

I turned angrily towards the genie. "You didn't tell me the price I would have to pay to have my wish fulfilled!"

The mouth in the genie's inhuman face opened in a disingenuous, mocking smile. "You never asked!"

The icon was quick to reproach her minion. "We are pure beings and it is our duty to treat the lower forms of existence with honesty and respect. Otherwise, we are no better than the demons that pay homage to Shiva." Again turning to me, Lakshmi asked, "Mortal, do you still wish to receive my gift?"

"No, Reverend Mother. I have been enlightened by your counsel and must regretfully decline it."

The icon regarded me with something akin to pity. "You have been misled and must be disappointed. I will grant you a token in place of the boon that you will not receive." The icon seized the lotus flower it held in one of its four hands, plucked a petal, and dropped it in my direction. As I bent to retrieve it, she added, "Keep this petal and ask for its guidance whenever you must make a difficult decision. It is true that wisdom comes with age and you have put your wisdom to good use today. The petal will not make you stronger, as you wished, but will render you even wiser.

"Now, both of you must depart in peace."

The moment the icon issued its dismissal the genie and I found ourselves in the square outside the temple.

* * *

"The Goddess granted you a boon. I will give you another, to make up for the disappointment I caused."

"What is your boon?" I asked, no longer trusting the deceitful creature.

"Since you are old and feeble, I will spare you the trip down the mountain. Close your eyes and think of the dwelling where you are staying."

I did as he ordered and immediately fell asleep.

Much later, I woke up in bed in a Lachung guest house. Had it all been a dream? Not likely, for I noticed that my right hand was clutching a crushed flower petal. Also, my knees and back hurt, as if I had recently engaged in strenuous activities.

And I remembered how, whether in a dream or in reality, I had been forced to take stock of my life and had decided that it had been fruitful and well worth the pains that old age was bringing. Rather than lamenting my departed youth, I would welcome the opportunity to live longer and become wiser, perhaps aided by the parting gift from a goddess.

Mid-morning light streamed through the window slats. Sadly, I had missed last night's Chaar mask dance event; I would have to try again next year, here or elsewhere.

Yet, I knew what my next travel chronicle must be: a *yatra*, a pilgrimage, to Lakshmi's temple in Kolhapur. I would join the Hindu faithful in paying homage to the deity and, in my case, give profound thanks.

Alas, during my flight to Mumbai, I suffered a major heart attack, from which I may not recover. As I lie in bed with death standing nearby, I can only wonder whether acceptance of the gift from the goddess would have been efficacious, despite her refusal to extend my lifespan, in prolonging my life and whether what I would have lost in experience and wisdom could have ever been recovered. However, only the gods know what lies in one's karma, and my questions must remain unanswered.

A Visit from the Jaguar

Quicemitqui in vollotl – The heat rules all.
- Nahuatl Proverb

"Flee, you say? Chalchiuhtolin must have nested in your head!" exclaimed Quetzalli in a shrill tone that departed from her usual demeanor.

"Not so" replied Cacalotl, ignoring the disrespect in his wife's words. "Afraid, yes. Desperate, yes. But crazy, no. I wish it were otherwise, but escaping is the only path that will deliver us and little Axochitl from a terrible death. Even as we speak, enemy forces are massing on the far shore of Lake Texcoco, getting ready to sail across the lake and launch a final assault on our city. Soon Azcapotzalco will be in ruins and all of us will be slain or taken into captivity and delivered to Tenochtitlan, where King Itzcoatl will surely ordain a massive human sacrifice to Huitzilopochtli. If we are taken, our chests will be sliced open and our still beating hearts will be offered to the God, and our blood will be spilled on the floor of the temple. Do you want that for us?"

"Of course not!" shuddered Quetzalli. "But surely Maxtla will defend us from the Aztecs!"

"Our Lord is fierce and wise," replied Cacalotl reverently. "But our forces are no match for the alliance that Itzcoatl has made with the Tlacopan traitors. No matter how valiantly we fight, we are sure to be defeated and captured."

"Holy Tonantzin, protect us!" implored Quetzalli, assuming her earlier shrill tone. Then, more soberly, "But how are we going to escape, and where are we going to go, and what are we going to do once we get there?"

"As to where, we must go west, towards the land of the Purépecha. Their empire is powerful and not likely to be overrun by our enemies. We would be safe there. I will work in the fields or become a fisherman as many of their folks are."

"And how do we get there?"

Cacolotl's voice became subdued. "We will have to travel on foot across the forests. It will be a long and difficult trip. There will be dangers."

"And you want to expose me and Axochitl to those dangers?"

"We have no choice. But I have a plan to get us some silver and maybe hire a warrior or two to accompany and defend us."

"What is your plan?"

"It may not work, but I'll try to get help from our gods. I'll just be gone a couple of days. Do you have enough food to last until I return?"

"For a couple of days, yes. I don't know what you mean by seeking help from the gods, but if you must go, please return as soon as you can."

* * *

The woods that massed behind Azcapotzalco were dense and had never been developed for human use, since the city's business was mainly with Lake Texcoco and the lands across from it. Cacolotl entered the forest after sunset and, as he stepped further onto the dirt path, he found himself surrounded by nothingness. There were no moon or stars showing in the cloudy night sky, and the pine torch Cacolotl carried barely illuminated the ground ahead of his feet. The only noises he could hear were the calls of night birds and the chirps of insects.

A feeling of impending doom seized his soul, and he began to head out of the woods, but then the unnatural silence was broken by a sudden crash, like the sound of a tree falling to the ground. As the reverberations from the crash subsided, a pair of huge gleaming eyes appeared a few paces ahead of where Cacolotl stood.

"What brings a human into this sacred forest when the rest of the world rests?" asked a roaring voice that was like the growl of a beast.

Cacolotl's terror was such that he was unable at first to utter a word. Then, regaining his voice, he responded, "Oh, Great Lord, I come in search of the Yoaltepuztli, who is said to dwell in this wilderness!"

The same voice returned, now in a less frightening tone. "I am Tecuani, the Jaguar. I am sometimes Yoaltepuztli's animal counterpart, his *nahual*, so that he can shapeshift into me when he so desires. But I also serve to house other beings besides the Lord of the Night Sky. What is your business with the Yoaltepuztli?"

"My family and I must flee this land before our soil is desecrated by an impending invasion by the Mexica. I am hoping to ask the Yoaltepuztli to assist us."

"Assist how?"

"Provide us with material means to carry out our escape."

"What makes you think he will do that?"

"It is said that if you are lucky enough to find the Yoaltepuztli and brave enough to approach him, he might be willing to grant your wishes."

"The Gods don't meddle in the affairs of men. Why would the Yoaltepuztli want to help you?"

"Because the Mexica, or the Aztecs as they call themselves, are a heathen race that knows only carnage and destruction. They will leave Azcapotzalco in ruins and annihilate its inhabitants, leaving no one to worship the Gods."

There was another thundering crash and a bright light filled the sky for a few seconds. The light vanished and with it went the glimmer of Tecuani's eyes, to be replaced by a phosphorescent human figure.

* * *

Yoaltepuztli was less terrifying than a jaguar would have been, yet its appearance was more awe-inspiring than that of any animal. It was humanoid in shape and somewhat taller than Cacolotl. That is, it would have been taller but for the fact that its body ended at its neck; a head was held in the left hand of the creature, hanging by a mass of greenish hairs that writhed like snakes. The most prominent feature in the head was a pair of gleaming eyes, identical to those displayed by Tecuani.

"You say you are seeking my help. Why do you deserve it?"

"I am a righteous man, who worships and reveres the Gods and will ensure wherever I go that the proper rituals and sacrifices are offered to honor them. If you help me escape, I will bring knowledge of our Gods to the land of the Purépecha, a vast empire many of whose citizens now live in sheer ignorance."

"Does your heart harbor any malice or any other weakness that would spoil its purity or diminish its quality?"

"No, Sire, my heart is strong and free of corruption. I am worthy of receiving your gifts."

"Very well, then," replied the Yoaltepuztli. There was a momentary silence, followed by the same crashing sound as before. This time, however, Cacolotl witnessed the origin of the sound: The creature had placed its head on the ground and, seizing its chest with both hands, was tearing it open to display its beating heart. Yoaltepuztli's response came out of its head, which remained on the ground.

"Gods have a need to periodically replenish their essence. Some, like Huitzilopochtli, require human sacrifices to maintain their powers. I purify myself by releasing my heart to a worthy human. Are you such a human, without fault or blame?"

"I am, O Lord," declared Cacolotl with as much conviction as he could muster.

"Well, then. You may approach and tear my heart out and carry it away with you."

"Do *what*?"

"You must seize my heart with your hands, twist it until it breaks, and hold it so you can carry it away."

"But... wouldn't that bring about your death?'

"Do not fear. A new heart will be in place tomorrow evening."

"Still, I don't dare touch your holy body."

The creature's voice was laden with sarcasm. "I thought you were a warrior, a brave man. Are you so craven as to be unable to pluck a heart that is proffered to you freely, like a ripe zapote hanging from a tree?"

Cacolotl became concerned he would be giving offense to Yoaltepuztli by refusing its offered heart and, with halting steps, approached the glowing figure, whose chest was now wide open with a pulsating heart very much in evidence. He brought his arms up, and, with some reluctance, inserted them into the cavity. He took hold of the organ and began twisting it, gently at first and then more forcefully. No blood or other fluids were shed, and the heart itself was warm and heavy, unresisting to his efforts.

After a few moments there was a snap and the heart dislodged itself from the cavity and came into Cacolotl's hands, who almost fell from the sudden release. He took a couple of steps back and asked, "Now what?"

The head replied, "Take off your cloak and wrap the heart inside it. You must take it back to your home and hold it out of sight for twenty-four hours without opening it while it assesses you and your claims. At the time an owl hoots tomorrow night, you will open the cloak and look inside. The heart will be gone, but inside will be my reward for your taking of my heart. If you have been truthful and steadfast, there will be treasures in place of the heart. If you have been proven weak or your account has been false, there will be only a collection of worthless pebbles. It will be best if you are alone when you look inside the cloak. Now, go!"

With that, Yoaltepuztli vanished into the air, leaving behind only a puff of acrid smoke.

* * *

The following night, Cacolotl sternly directed his wife to spend the night with her mother, for he needed to be alone to perform a special ritual to the Gods. Quetzalli was puzzled by the order, but knew better than to disobey her husband when he used that commanding tone of voice with her.

Alone, Cacolotl went to the family shrine where the images of the Gods were kept and retrieved the cloak he had hidden there. He sat on the floor by the door of his home, waiting for the characteristic trill of an owl's hoot. Just as that signal arrived, there was a growl outside, and a moment later Tecuani materialized inside the house.

Cacolotl had not been able to make out Tecuani's shape in the previous night's darkness. This time, however, the light of the torches inside the dwelling revealed an imposing sight. Tecuani was easily twice the size of a grown man and had a muscled body, tan/orange in color with hollow black markings in the form of rosettes on its back and solid black markings on the white underside. It had large yellow eyes that squinted, giving it a cruel, pitiless appearance. Its large, sharp teeth gleamed as in expectation of its next meal. Cacolotl reckoned that Tecuani could finish him in just a couple of bites.

"Yoaltepuztli cannot come because it is still waiting for his new heart, so it sent me to watch you open the cloak," explained the Jaguar.

Cacolotl placed the cloak on the ground and opened it carefully. Its contents were puzzling: there were some ornaments made of gold and silver, pieces of jade and turquoise stones, and a few colorful feathers of quetzals and hummingbirds. However, the rest of the contents of the cloak were black pebbles, obviously worthless.

"What is this?" questioned Cacolotl.

"That is your reward, measured from your evaluation by Yoaltepuztli's old heart. It found that you were brave in seeking Yoaltepuztli's assistance and were not deterred by its nonhuman appearance. You are also loving and faithful to your family and loyal to your human lord. Yet you lied repeatedly: you falsely accused the Mexica of impiety, falsely claimed that you are wanting to go away in order to propagate the faith in the Gods in a place where such faith is lacking, and hid your fear that you may become a sacrificial offering. There are also other hidden flaws that you did not mention, such as your dishonesty towards others with whom you do business. In sum, your heart holds a mixture of good and evil, but such is the case with the hearts of all humans. That mixture is reflected in the bounty you have received—the worth of a heart like yours."

The Jaguar then approached Cacolotl threateningly. "But now it is time to go. The Yoaltepuztli waits for your heart."

A chill ran down Cacolotl's spine. "What do you mean?"

"Your heart is to replace the one you took away last night. Yours is far from perfect, but will serve until the next one comes around to replace it."

The Jaguar leapt and, in three bites, extracted Cacolotl's heart and bit it off the vessels to which it was connected.

Cacolotl had only time for one thought as the Jaguar's jaws closed on his chest. *I hope the reward for my heart will be enough to pay for my family's escape!*

Then all his cares abruptly ended.

YOSSELE IN LOVE

Everyone says it's a myth until one day something happens in the streets that brings it back to life.
- Gustav Meyrink, *The Golem*

"**M**y counselors tell me you are the most knowledgeable man in all of Europe on matters relating to the Kabbalah, isn't that so?" questioned Emperor Rudolf II, speaking cheerfully to the bearded old man that stood before him in the Prague Castle's reception room.

"I am only a humble student," replied the man, bowing his head. "My ignorance in all matters, human as well as divine, is vast." He shrugged his shoulders in self-deprecation.

"You are Judah Loew ben Bezalel, the most famous rabbi in Prague. I desire to master the practical arts that can be gleaned from the Kabbalah, and want you to lend me your firm hand, guide me away from any perilous undertakings. Will you lend me your assistance in this?"

"I must point out the dangerous nature of the knowledge you seek. However, I am willing to teach Your Majesty some of the practical aspects of the Kabbalah, but I would ask in exchange for an important boon for my people."

"What would that be?"

"Jews all over the Empire, and particularly in this city of Prague, are being unjustly persecuted on account of a slanderous tale that is being bandied about."

"What tale is this?"

"They say that we Jews murder innocent children and drain their blood to be used as an ingredient in the preparation of matzah and wine for our Passover services. This is a horrific lie, but one that has cost the lives of many of my people."

"I expect this is only another old wives' tale spread by the ignorant."

"I wish it were so. Actually a prominent priest named Thaddeus is spreading this libelous tale among his parishioners and egging them on against us."

"What do you want me to do?"

"Punish Thaddeus for spreading false rumors and prohibit dissemination of the libel."

"I can't do that. The Holy Roman Empire is a Christian nation. I can't take your side against the vast majority of my subjects. It is regrettable that people are acting in such a manner, but the Jews need to find a way to protect themselves without my help."

"Do you authorize us to take defensive measures against those who attack us?"

"Yeah. Form a militia or something. As long as you don't engage the authorities or damage public property, I will not interfere with your acts in self-defense."

"Thank you, Your Majesty. I think we have an understanding. When would you want to receive instruction on the Kabbalah?"

***

Rabbi Loew spent several days rereading the sacred texts and meditating. He was unwilling to create an armed militia for fear of causing widespread bloodshed. His heart rebelled against another course of action that kept suggesting itself, for it required him to assume powers that only God possessed; but Rudolf's equivocal support for limited actions to protect the Jewish population of Prague left Loew without an alternative.

One night in March he went to the shore of the Moldau in the company of two younger men, his son Bezalel and Yaakov, a disciple, and dug out a large amount of mud from the banks of the river and carried it in buckets back to the Old-New Synagogue in the heart of Prague's Jewish Town. They brought the buckets to the attic, and there the three men labored all night to mold the wet mud into an enormous human-like figure, with massive arms and legs and a misshapen head with two holes for eyes, no nose or ears, and a mouth that was only a wide slit.

Contemplating their handiwork, Loew declared: "This lump of mud is like Adam before being instilled with the spark of life. It's a golem, an unfinished creation. Let's attempt to animate it."

Loew inserted in the mouth slit of the giant a piece of parchment in which were inscribed the letters "chet" and "yud," spelling the symbol for "life"; he and his disciples danced three times clockwise around the prone figure of the golem, each time repeating aloud those letters, at the end of which Loew whispered the secret name of God.

The creature on the ground shuddered, rose to its feet, and stood immobile before its astonished audience. There was long silence.

Loew then stood next to the golem and uttered a summoning in the firm voice he used when addressing his congregation. "Golem, I am your creator and master. Henceforth you will obey my every command. Your name shall be Josef, although I and others may address you as Yossele. Bend your head to signify your understanding!"

The golem slowly lowered its head and issued a low grunt.

"I shall teach you how to speak if I can," continued Loew. "You'll also learn your household duties and other actions that you will need to take on my behalf. Right now, remain standing and do not move until I command you to do so."

Yossele became a statue whose head almost touched the low ceiling of the attic.

"Let's go down," Loew directed Bezalel and Yaakov. "We have a lot of planning to do. Passover is only weeks away."

* * *

As the holiday approached, Rabbi Loew and his assistants set in motion a plan to protect the inhabitants of Prague's Jewish Town from attacks by Christian extremists and hoodlums. The rabbi's wife, Perle, fashioned a large, hooded wrap that covered Yossele's body except its arms and served to mask its figure from the casual attention of most passersby. Bezalel would lead the golem in a nightly pilgrimage through the streets of Prague, and if they became aware of an actual or threatened attack by outsiders against inhabitants of Jewish Town, Bezalel would order, "Yossele, go get them!" and motion the golem to lunge at the attackers and drive them off.

There were four such encounters; in each instance, Yossele ignored the clubs, knives, and other weapons of the marauders and cracked heads, broke limbs, and tossed bodies to the ground with mechanical thoroughness, only stopping when Bezalel blew a whistle whose harsh and grating sound caused the golem to return to Bezalel's side, leaving the results of the carnage behind. All told, Yossele slew ten attackers and wounded an unknown number of others, and its exploits became legendary, both among the Jews and the other inhabitants of the city.

At the end of each night's promenade, Bezalel would lead the golem back to the Old-New Synagogue and take it to the attic. Loew would then issue the command, "Sleep now!" and remove the parchment from Yossele's mouth, rendering it immobile until the next time the golem needed to be awakened, which was done by reinsertion of the parchment and issuance of the command, "Awake!"

Loew would spend such time as his other duties permitted teaching Yossele to understand common speech, as well as training the golem to follow silent commands by imitating the gestures of the rabbi, his wife and children, and his disciples. Yossele proved to have very low intelligence, but was docile and performed the ordered chores capably, although it had to be directed to stop repetitive tasks when the assigned activity was completed, else Yossele would have continued to carry out the work.

***

Passover seders and other religious observances were peacefully conducted in Prague that year and many others to come, as the legend of the avenging monster spread throughout the Holy Roman Empire; Jewish mothers began telling their children tales about the friendly monster that protected them and their families from attacks by the *goyim*. A new type of gingery "golem biscuit" in the approximate shape of Yossele was created and became a delicacy for the residents and visitors of Prague for centuries to come. It was all for the good.

***

One night, Loew was busy writing one of his sermons and asked Perle to put Yossele to sleep after Bezalel and the golem returned from their night rounds. It was well past midnight when Bezalel returned, took the golem to the attic, and went to sleep himself. By that time, Perle had forgotten her assignment and retired, leaving the golem in the attic, unattended and awake.

A few hours later, some noise outside the premises rendered Yossele restless. The golem went down the steps to the main room of the temple, let itself out, and, as it had seen Bezalel do many times, steered itself through the narrow streets of the Jewish Town. It was almost daybreak and the streets were deserted, so Yossele ambled aimlessly in the dark without meeting anyone, until the light in a building drew its attention. A small establishment, a bakery, was already open as the baker and his assistants busied themselves preparing babka, rugelach, challah, and mandelbrot for the morning trade. Yossele lacked the sense of smell, but was attracted by the light of the candles and the firing ovens and tumbled into the establishment by shoving the door open and approaching the counter with heavy steps.

Bedlam followed. The baker and his assistants ran in panic to hide in a back room; only a young girl, who dispensed the merchandise to the buyers, stayed behind the counter, rigid with fear. Yossele approached her and, having received no instructions to attack, stood staring at the girl curiously. She was rather plain—one would even call her ugly—but the golem was mesmerized by her youthful appearance.

For a moment, neither moved. Then the girl, who was accustomed to dealing with all sorts of customers, grinned and said, "Hello! I'm Havah! How can I help you?" She had a musical voice and a practiced, friendly manner that Yossele already associated with the members of Rabbi Loew's family, so the golem sensed kinship and grunted back in a nonthreatening tone.

Havah had heard the rumors about the existence of a protecting golem, and this creature seemed to fit the description that was circulating around town. She turned towards the back room and shouted, "Master Arieh! Send someone quickly to the Synagogue and fetch Rabbi Loew! I think we have gotten his golem here!"

Then, facing the unexpected guest, Havah said in her sweetest voice, "May I offer you a piece of challah? It is fresh out of the oven!" She tore a piece of bread and, with slow, deliberate gestures, tendered it to Yossele.

The golem reached for the bread, seized it, and dropped it to the floor. It issued another grunt and remained standing, eyes fixed on the girl.

Havah then launched into a low tone monologue in which she recited, in the calmest, friendliest voice, everything that came to her mind, from the history of her family to the names of her friends and her favorite games and activities, and the songs she sang and prayers she chanted when she attended Sabbath services. The door to the shop then opened and a disheveled, sleepy-eyed Rabbi Loew entered and took command of the situation.

* * *

Things appeared to go back to normal after the incident, but Loew sensed they were not so. Yossele still obeyed his orders, performed menial tasks like fetching logs for firewood and protective ones like cracking the heads of hostile *goyim*, but there was a new hesitation every time the rabbi or any of his family members addressed the golem with a new command. Finally, Loew decided to get at the roots of the problem and questioned Yossele.

"Josef, you have been created to serve the rightful needs of man, but you seem to bridle at receiving our commands. Express what is in your mind, so it can be put to rest! Speak now!"

The rabbi did not expect that Yossele would utter any words, for the golem did not have the gift of speech. However, he was taken aback by the creature's response. Yossele walked unsteadily to the back wall, where hung a painting of Abraham and his family, and stabbed with a stubby finger at one of the figures in the background: Sarah, the patriarch's wife. While it did this, Yossele emitted a different sort of grunt than its usual utterances: a moaning sound that suggested desire and longing.

It took Loew a few moments to comprehend the golem's lament, but when understanding struck him the rabbi gasped in astonishment. "You desire a woman!"

Yossele nodded gravely.

"But that cannot be..." started the rabbi, and caught himself. "Yossele, I can perhaps make another creature to be your companion, but golems are neither male nor female, and my next creation would be just a replica of yourself. Another Yossele. Is that what you want?"

Golems are unable to voice their emotions, but Yossele rejected the rabbi's offer by striking the wall forcefully, leaving a large crack in the plaster, and grunting loudly.

"I'm sorry, Yossele, but there is no way I can make you a female companion! Even the Lord could not create a woman directly, but had to fashion one from Adam's rib. And you have no ribs that I could modify to make a female golem!"

Yossele did not understand the joke, but by now it could read a person's expression and negation and regret were written clearly on the old rabbi's face. The golem issued another loud grunt and stood still, awaiting its orders.

* * *

Three mornings later, Perle had just slid the magical parchment in Yossele's mouth and was starting to direct the golem to fetch water from the community well when the golem pushed her aside and bounded down the attic stairs, across the temple's main room, and out into the street. Perle was flabbergasted, and then frightened. A rebellious golem was outside her expectation. Finally, she shook herself and ran over to the bedroom, where Loew still rested in bed. "Husband, something terrible has happened! Yossele has run away!"

The rabbi was immediately awake at the sound of the news. "Wake Bezalel up!" he commanded, threw some clothes on, and ran down the stairs and out the front door.

Outside, there was a clamor, as people were talking loudly and gesticulating. "Which way did he go?" shouted the rabbi. Three people pointed in the direction of the market at the center of Jewish Town, and Loew bolted in that direction without giving thanks.

Four blocks later, Loew found himself in front of the Jewish bakery where he had retrieved Yossele a fortnight before. The wooden door had been torn off its hinges and three men were cowering, their backs to the walls. Yossele was holding Havah by the arm, and the girl, white with fear, was uttering some nonsense, calming words.

Loew issued a stern command at the top of his voice, "Josef, let go of that girl!"

The golem turned to face him and for a moment it seemed as if it was about to attack the rabbi. Then, very slowly, it let go of Havah's hand and stood before its master.

What followed was perhaps the most courageous act in the rabbi's life. He came forward and yanked the magic parchment out of the golem's mouth, an act that might have cost him his life had Yossele resisted. But the golem allowed its master to assert his authority, and stood frozen in the middle of the shop, which by now was filled with Bezalel and others.

It took four men to carry the golem's motionless body back to the Old-New Synagogue and up the stairs to the attic, where they lay Yossele on the floor.

"What shall we do with him?" asked Bezalel. "Should we destroy him, or undo the enchantment that created him?"

Loew was overcome with emotion. He shook his head. "It is not Yossele's fault, but mine. I let my pride convince me I could replicate the Lord's handiwork. I succeeded, but gave Yossele feelings that cannot be satisfied. He fell in love with a girl! I must now try to find a way to remedy the ill that I have caused to a guiltless creature. For now, wrap Yossele's body in prayer shawls and keep it hidden in the attic, asleep. I will hopefully think of what to do."

But Rabbi Loew could never find the answer, and Yossele still remains asleep in that attic, perhaps dreaming of a girl that only he could find beautiful. Only heaven knows what would happen were he ever to awaken.

CARAWAY SEED CAKE

A seed neither fears light nor darkness,
but uses both to grow.
- Matshona Dhliwayo

It was a long haul from Capitol Hill to his walkup apartment near Florida Avenue, but that mid-September afternoon Chester Cassidy felt too full of himself to notice the hike.

His mind was occupied with the new project he had been assigned as he entered H Street and found himself walking through a raucous crowd. This was strange, as this part of town was usually deserted on Saturday afternoons to become repopulated later in the evening. Then he realized it was the H Street Festival, an annual extravaganza that went on for block after block of music stages, merchandise stands, artist exhibitions, and food trucks and stalls.

He bought a can of soda from a truck and began strolling through the milling crowds. As he did, he realized he was a little hungry and in the mood for a snack.

He stopped in front of a table set up by a wrinkled black woman wearing a cloth skirt and a strange head wrap made of intertwined cords. The table displayed a variety of baked goods, some which looked appetizing; others were unrecognizable. He pointed to a slice of black forest cake and asked, "How much for that?"

"Two dollah," replied the woman in a heavy foreign accent.

His mind was still racing through the new assignment. "Where are you from?" he asked in an accusatory tone.

The woman was startled and shuddered a little before responding, "I'm from Maridi."

"Where is that?" he pressed, increasing the menace in his voice.

"In the country you call South Sudan," she allowed, in a pained sort of way.

Chester's thoughts turned again to his new assignment. South Sudan was one of the targets of the aid cutting project the Senator had assigned to him: humanitarian aid to that country must be cut for it was going to waste in a country racked by violence, disease, flooding, and other natural and manmade disasters. Those thoughts spilled into the next words he uttered. "You escape your hellhole of a country, manage to land in America, and try to get rich at our expense!"

The old woman's eyebrows rose and her nose wrinkled in surprise, or perhaps fear. She responded quickly. "No, sir, I no steal from you!"

Chester felt reassured he was dealing with an inferior being and decided to have fun. "Yeah, that is all you wetbacks say. You sneak into America and start taking everything that ain't nailed down!" he asserted loudly.

The woman blanched but said nothing. She may have thought his tirade referred to the price of the cake, for she turned around and rummaged through a basket behind the table. She produced a plastic-wrapped yellow-brown square of crumbly cake from which protruded a multitude of black seeds. "Here, this one for one dollah!"

Chester thought of correcting the woman's misunderstanding, but the cake she proffered looked interesting. "What are those black things, seeds?"

"Caraway seeds."

Chester took out a dollar bill and tossed it to the woman. She inserted it inside her blouse and looked at him inquisitively, in case he was going to demand something else. Chester shook his head with contempt and walked on.

As he moved through the festival crowd, Chester unwrapped the cake and took a bite. The dessert had a pungent, anise-like flavor emanating from the seeds. He did not care for licorice, so he considered throwing the rest of the cake away, but then other competing tastes assaulted him: citrus, fragrant woods, some earthy aroma he felt he knew but could not place. He decided it was too unique a taste experience to miss and kept on eating, bite after bite, so the entire pastry was consumed before he had advanced another block.

He still had an unpleasant fennel taste in his mouth when he arrived in his apartment, so he poured himself a glass of rough California chardonnay to wash it off. He had his usual TV dinner, watched some porn, and called it a day.

***

Stabs of pain emanating from his stomach woke Chester up in the middle of the night. He ran to the bathroom seeking to relieve himself, but was unsuccessful. The pain was planted firmly, right in the middle of his gut, and gave no signs of abatement. He drank a full bottle of water and ate a banana, and these caused his stomach to begin churning but provided no relief. There was nothing in his medicine cabinet that would seem to help, and the pain was getting worse, so he threw some clothes on and ran to the twenty-four-hour drugstore a couple of blocks away.

There, he walked right up to the pharmacy counter and woke up a dozing clerk. "Please, I need quick help. I have this excruciating pain in my stomach. What do you have for that?"

The woman yawned and replied, "Look in Aisle 9, where we keep the stomach discomfort products. The best thing we carry is called 'Stomach Relief – Maximum Strength.' It comes in a large pink bottle..." The clerk was still talking when Chester bounded for Aisle 9 and began searching frantically for the medication. There was just one bottle of the stomach relief liquid. He seized and returned to the clerk.

"Can I pay you for this?"

As she was running the sale through the credit card reader, Chester asked, "Do you have any plastic cups I can borrow?"

She shrugged her shoulders. "Sorry, no." She returned the card and added, "But you can sit right there and drink it out of the bottle, if you wish."

Chester grabbed the bottle and sat on a chair near the counter. He violently tore the plastic cover off the bottle, yanked the cap, and took three big gulps of the thick, viscous liquid. As he swallowed, he anticipated that relief would soon arrive. He threw his head back against the wall and relaxed.

When the medication coursed down his esophagus and reached his stomach, he was assaulted by a sense of revulsion that made him instantly feel like throwing up. He hurried to the bathroom, where he vomited the pink liquid in a series of spasmodic discharges. As he did, a thought assaulted him. *Whatever is in there does not want to be disturbed.*

He tossed the useless bottle of medication in the trash can and walked out of the store.

* * *

As he rushed back to his apartment, Chester felt the pain in stomach worsen, to the point he could hardly breathe. He needed help, quickly. He changed course and headed for the nearest hospital, a couple of miles away, hoping to be able to make it before he fainted from the pain. The streets of the city were deserted as it was past three a.m. on a Sunday morning, but by a stroke of luck he noticed a taxicab approaching from the opposite direction. He went onto the street and started to wave his arms frantically to attract the driver's attention. The car stopped and he ran across the road, opened the back door of the taxi, and collapsed inside, whispering with his last breath, "Take me to the ER, please!"

A few minutes later he found himself in an emergency room full of the casualties of weekend partying: the wounded, the drug overdose cases, the drunks. As he filled the admission form, he realized his emergency was probably less severe than those of the unfortunates surrounding him, but the pain he was suffering was no less intense.

"Please, I need to be seen right away! I am in excruciating pain!" he implored.

The nurse looked up and noticed Chester's sweating and agitation and the extreme pallor on his face. "I'll see if I can get you a bed."

Getting a bed in a crowded emergency room is always time consuming, and it was almost an hour before Chester was led to a cubicle, empty except for a narrow bed and a chair. He lay down, breathing with difficulty, and begged the nurse, "Please give me an injection! This pain is killing me!"

They eventually hooked Chester to an IV pole and administered a dose of Ketorolac, which reduced the pain but did not erase it entirely; Chester continued to feel as if something was gnawing at his stomach, taking a bite at a time. He closed his eyes and descended into a stupor.

Arrival of a doctor brought him back to reality. The doctor, reading the details of Chester's medical history, asked breezily, "So, you are experiencing severe stomach pain. Is this the first time your tummy hurts like this?"

Chester felt some irritation at the condescending question, but replied as briefly as he could, "First time. I've never been sick a day in my life."

"What did you have for dinner?"

"A frozen fried chicken TV dinner."

"Anything unusual about it?"

"No. It just tasted like cardboard."

"And to drink?"

"A beer."

"Nothing else to eat or drink in the last twenty-four hours?"

"I had lunch on the Hill. I work there. I had a hamburger and fries, and a Diet Coke."

"Anything unusual about your lunch?"

"No. The hamburger was overcooked and the fries were soggy, but that's the way they always are."

"Anything else to eat or drink?"

The question brought to Chester's mind the African street vendor. "Oh, I had a piece of seed cake from a street vendor. Just a snack."

"And are you in pain now?"

"Yes, but not as much as before. I still feel there is something inside me."

"Well, we'll run some tests, like blood, stool and urine, but we may need to take a good look at what's going on. We may need an MRI of the stomach area."

"Whatever you have to do. My pay as a Congressional Staff member is low, but I have good health insurance."

"We'll keep you here and run the tests. By later tonight we should know what we have."

* * *

Hours later, a visibly disturbed doctor walked into the holding room where Chester had lingered since his arrival at the ER.

"All your tests came out negative; blood, urine, stool, are all normal. But..." The doctor paused, as if he was having trouble getting his words out. "The MRI shows something very odd."

"What is that?"

"It looks as if you have things growing in your stomach."

"Like a cancer?"

"No, these things are not part of your own body but some foreign matter."

"What do you mean?"

"The human stomach has several layers of tissue; the innermost is the mucosa, a membrane where the acid is generated to digest the food. Around that mucosa is another layer, the submucosa, that contains blood vessels and nerve cells. Next is the main muscle of the stomach, wrapped inside a thin strong membrane that confines the organ and holds it in place. The MRI shows many small dark items adhered to the mucosa, some of which seem to be penetrating the mucosa and the submucosa and reaching into the muscular layer. That intrusion into the muscle layer is probably what causes your pain."

"Do you mean those things are drilling holes on my stomach from the inside?"

"We don't understand the mechanism, but that is perhaps as good a description as any."

"But what are those things?"

"We don't know yet. We'll have to consult a specialist."

* * *

They put Chester under anesthesia so they could make small incisions on his body and find and remove some of the pieces of foreign matter for analysis. The results were astonishing. Under the microscope, the dark pieces were shown to be caraway seeds that had taken hold on the inner surface of the stomach and had germinated quickly. Then the little plants had drilled through the stomach's membranes and sunk their rootlets into the rich outlying muscular tissue.

"He appears to be growing caraway plants in his stomach. I have no idea how that is even possible, but it's happening," concluded the doctor.

When Chester recovered from his astonishment, he asked the obvious question. "How are you going to get rid of those things? Are you going to open me up and take them out one by one?"

"That would be risky and perhaps unfeasible. The MRI showed that some of the seeds appear to be close to breaking through the stomach's outer membrane, allowing digestive juices and food to leak into the abdominal cavity. That would call for immediate removal of all or part of your stomach. At the same time, if plants break through, they may travel within your abdominal cavity, so they could be poised to take root in other major organs—liver, kidneys, even heart—and their removal could prove fatal."

"So, what am I going to do?"

"You have three choices: first, do nothing and await the inevitable; second, undergo a very risky operation from which you may not survive; and third, maintain yourself in as good a physical shape as possible while the medical community investigates ways of removing the seeds safely."

Chester realized he most likely was going to die, and his death would be an exceedingly painful process. He could be given painkillers and be provided with palliative care, but the end was inevitable and would happen in the not-too-distant future.

"I'll take the last option," he declared. "I'm going to fight this to the end."

But, in the meantime, he would try to figure out how he got in this predicament, and come up with a way to fix it if the doctors could not do it themselves.

The image of the old black woman who sold him the seed cake kept recurring in his thoughts. He took a medical leave of absence from his senator's office, barricaded himself in his apartment, and devoted every hour of each increasingly painful day to doing research about South Sudan.

He had forgotten where in the country the woman was from, but her peculiar appearance provided some help in identifying her. From articles he consulted and pictures he saw he learned that some members of an ethnic group known as the Azande wear headgear made of ropes to preclude malevolent spirits from penetrating their brains. Other facts seemed to confirm that the Azande were the right group to investigate: their area of the country was impoverished and subject to flooding and other disasters, and after South Sudan's secession from Sudan, a number of

Azande had been given humanitarian visas allowing them to migrate to the United States.

The next step in his research was contacting the organizers of the H Street Festival to find out the identity of the woman who had rented space for a table during the festival. With some effort, he learned that space for a table to sell food and souvenirs from "Central Africa" had been leased to a Boukrine Angbapio from somewhere in Virginia. The lessee paid in cash, so no bank records existed of the transaction.

Through his state department contacts, Chester ran a parallel investigation of the INS records to determine whether immigration records existed for a Boukrine Angbapio. No such records existed. But the State Department was helpful in a different way: a staffer at the South Sudan desk of the department put him in contact with Achol "Daisy" Lokonyen, an employee of the South Sudan Embassy in Washington. Daisy, a middle-aged woman with an amiable face, agreed to meet with Chester.

Their meeting did not go well. He was curt and condescending, but she took pity on his dire circumstances and agreed to help him locate the caraway seed cake vendor.

"A thing that you must understand is that witchcraft is prevalent among the Azande. The woman who gave you that cake is most likely a witch, and because of her advanced age, a powerful one. Witches like her operate by sending out a spirit, a bodiless messenger of their own witchcraft, to perform their evil deed upon her intended victim. In your case, she was probably at home asleep when the spirit she summoned caused the caraway seeds in your stomach to become active and start eating you away from within. We need to be very careful on how we deal with this woman if we find her."

"We *have* to find her," pressed Chester. "I am in more pain each day and have been seen by every doctor in the city, and no one can do anything for me. I can't sleep more than a few minutes at a time. I'm dying horribly. How can we find that witch?"

"With some difficulty," she conceded. "The way to find a South Sudanese needle in the big haystack of the Washington, D.C. area is to become aware of the public events held by our community. The largest number of South Sudanese around here live in Alexandria, Virginia, and their events may be advertised in the Alexandria local papers. Let us look through the Alexandria Gazette Package and see what we find."

After a search, they found a small advertisement placed by the South Sudanese Association for a charity event that had taken place at a local church a couple of months before. The ad asked for food donations in support of the gathering. Daisy volunteered to call both the association and the church to make inquiries about donors of food, particularly desserts, for that event. She struck gold: a secretary at the association remarked that an old widow who lived in one of Alexandria's poor neighborhoods was a frequent donor of home baked desserts for association events. She gave Daisy a name, Atonita Malual, and an address at a low-income apartment building.

"They probably would not have given any information to a condescending gringo like you, but I am one of their number, so they opened up to me," bragged Daisy.

"Very good!" replied Chester, ignoring the rebuke. "Let's go, now! My stomach is literally killing me!"

"Not so fast," replied Daisy. "She will probably deny having bewitched you. We need proof."

"What sort of proof?"

"The Azande use divination methods or 'oracles' to determine whether a person is guilty of witchcraft. These days, the method they most commonly use is consultation by cutting the neck of a chicken while posing the question whether a person is a witch; if the answer is yes, the dying chicken falls with its left wing topmost, and if the answer is no, it falls with its right wing topmost... Alternatively, they go to the *Nagidi*, a prophetess. One goes to her and explains the matter, and she dreams about it. The dream will tell her whether the accused is guilty of witchcraft or innocent."

"Do we have to kill a chicken or hire a prophetess to find out whether that Atonita is a witch?"

"Hopefully not. It may be sufficient to threaten her with doing this to get her to confess."

"Isn't threatening the woman sort of taking a big chance?"

"We have nothing else to go on. So, we have to try it."

* * *

Atonita Malual lived in a one-bedroom apartment in a low-income housing project. She opened the door to Daisy when they knocked, but her eyes widened upon recognizing the young white man that accompanied her. The old woman stepped back in fright at the couple of visitors, but allowed them in.

They sat on a worn-out sofa while she occupied a chair across from them. As they talked, Chester noticed the dilapidated condition of the apartment: there were holes in the walls and the floor appeared to be buckling. Water stains dotted the carpet, and the slats on the blinds of the window were cracked. There was a noticeable smell of decaying or rancid food that permeated the apartment.

"Mrs. Malual, my name is Achol Lokonyen," stated Daisy, assuming an official tone. "I am an official of the South Sudan Embassy in this country, and have been asked to investigate a complaint against you."

"A complain? I done nothin wrong. All my papers are in order."

"The complaint is not about your papers. Do you know this man?" She pointed to Chester.

"I seen him a few weeks ago at the Festival."

"Didn't you have an altercation with him?"

"What's dat?"

"I mean a fight."

"No fight. But he treated me bad. Called me names."

"Did he make you angry?"

"Angry no, but very upset."

"Did you feel like he had to be punished?"

"Nooo. But maybe he deserved."

"Did you sell him some pastry?"

"Yeah, a cheap piece of leftover cake, the butt of a bar I baked."

"Caraway seed cake?"

"Yeah. I make my mother's recipe."

"That's the problem. He ate that cake and is now very sick. The caraway seeds in that cake are eating him from the inside."

Atonita's face drained of color and she started to shake. "Can't be. I sold pieces of that cake to several people, and ate a slice myself. Nobody harmed."

"That doesn't prove anything," insisted Daisy. "The cake in itself may have been fine, but if you are a witch, you may have sent an evil spirit that caused the caraway seeds to start growing in this man's stomach."

"*I no witch!*" bellowed the old woman. "I'm poor woman living on pension! Never did harm to nobody!"

Daisy was unmoved. "You may not know you are a witch. Witchcraft resides in *mangu*, a substance in the witch's belly, inherited from a parent of the same sex. The substance leads a life of its own and can independently afflict people, especially those with whom the witch has a disagreement. You may have powerful *mangu* in you and may be unaware, but it may have sensed your anger at this man and may have acted to harm him."

"I no witch!" repeated Atonita.

"We can get a *Nagidi*, a prophetess, to dream up the answer to the question whether you have a *mangu* that harmed Mr. Cassidy here. If her dream answer is yes, you may end up in jail."

"Nooo, I don't wanna go to jail!" Atonita wrung her hands, breaking up in tears. "Is there a thing I can do?"

"I have looked into this," replied Daisy. "The practice is that once the person committing an act of witchcraft has been found, the victim will confront the witch and ask her to stop the witchcraft. The witch will then make amends by expressing her goodwill toward the victim and asking the *mangu* to cease its attack. Are you willing to do this, and do it sincerely?"

"Yeah, I never meant no harm to dis man."

They went through the reconciliation steps, and Chester and Atonita ended up embracing each other. For once, he was even sincere in his feeling of gratitude towards the dark woman.

As they left the apartment, Chester asked, "Do you think it will work?"

"Let's hope so," replied Daisy.

* * *

The *mangu* apparently ceased, prompting the caraway seeds to spread further into Chester's body, but the damage had been done already. The injuries to Chester's stomach were analogous to that caused by severe stomach ulcers and were so numerous that a gastrectomy had to be performed and much of the organ had to be removed. Recovery from the operation was slow and very painful, and the quality of Chester's life was irreparably affected.

Chester was still struggling to regain a normal life three years after the operation. He had aged prematurely and no longer harbored hopes of pursuing a career in Capitol Hill or anywhere else in the public light. He became a recluse and never married.

Several thoughts kept haunting him. He blamed himself for his arrogance. He lamented the suffering he had experienced and the still lingering effects of the attack from the malignant seeds. He took some comfort from his decision to fight his condition and his perseverance in continuing to struggle through years of agony, but lamented that full success in defeating the malevolent spell was never to be achieved.

He was grateful to be alive. He lived frugally and ate sparingly, for his stomach gave him no peace. And he never ate cake again.

ATONEMENT

The truth is you can never truly make amends
For the hurt you cause;
You apologize, you try to atone,
at best the scars lighten but they don't disappear.
- Justin A. Reynolds, *Early Departures*

What caused the accident? The night was dark, there was a rising fog, the country road was curvy, and Jeder was driving a bit too fast and perhaps had downed one cocktail too many at the party. Whether any or all these factors contributed, the GMC Sierra pickup truck left the pavement, broke through the surrounding shrubs and boulders, flew for some seconds through the air, and plunged with a crash into the muddy creek below. Jeder was dead on impact, crushed against the steering wheel, as he was wearing no seatbelt.

A resonance, like a voice emanating from the void, beckoned him. "Come, spirit, for you are to be assessed."

Jeder's spirit did not react well to the summons. "I can't go yet. I left things unfinished, matters that require my attention. I must go back."

There was no anger or irony in the response from the resonance. "Most say that. Death finds most humans unready. But the affairs of the living take care of themselves, despite the absence of the departed."

Jeder's spirit wrung its nonexistent hands in distress. "Not in this case. There are important things that will not be resolved unless my living body takes care of them!"

"What things are these that cannot be dealt with by others in your absence?"

"I need my body back to remember them exactly. But I know they are crucial!" Jeder's spirit fragmented and reformed rapidly, mimicking the motions of a living man convulsing with anguish.

There was a long pause, as if the unseen presence was considering matters or consulting with another. At the end, the resonance sounded again. "Very well. Your distress is severe and must be tempered if your soul is to be properly assessed. You will be returned to life at a moment twenty-four hours ago. You will retain the urgency you now have of addressing those pending matters that are so important. Whether or not you resolve them, your spirit will return at this time and place once the day is over."

* * *

When Jeder woke up again, he took a long, hot shower, shaved and groomed carefully, and dressed in casual, if fashionable clothes: a Zegna cashmere coat, Zanella trousers, Louboutin loafers. By the time his toilette was complete, the sun had risen above the horizon and he felt hungry. He got in his truck and drove to a nearby café, where he picked up a copy of the *Wall Street Journal* and ordered his favorite breakfast: a lumberjack omelet, pancakes, juice, and coffee. He leisurely consumed the food, drank two cups of coffee, and skimmed through the news of the world through the paper's conservative filter.

Once breakfast was over, Jeder set to the task of planning his day. He had recently retired from work at age fifty-five, after a successful career as an investment banker had left him with more money than he could expect to spend, since he was divorced and his ex-wife and children were on their own. He had no pressing duties and had scrupulously avoided committing himself to the political engagements that often come to people of his status. He was free as a bird, without obligations or demands on his time or re-sources.

Jeder was in the process of deciding whether to go play some tennis when disquiet disrupted his planning. Was he not supposed to do something important today? Try as he might, however, nothing was coming to mind, even though the nagging feeling of urgency remained.

He placed a call and made an appointment with the tennis instructor at his country club for an hour hence. To kill some time, he went to the Barnes & Noble outlet in the shopping mall to see if the next thriller by his favorite mass-market author had arrived. The book was not in yet, so he ambled through the stalls looking for something not too demanding to read.

Finally, it was time for his tennis lesson. Jeder played absently, his mind elsewhere, and once the lesson was over, he sat in the members' lounge and tried to elicit from his slippery mind the task that continued to elude him. It was getting close to lunch time, and an idea occurred to him: he would call his one-time flame Carmela and invite her to break bread and perhaps spend some quality time together at her apartment. They had dated years before, but their relationship had turned by mutual consent into a stream of casual encounters. She remained the equivalent of doing the crossword puzzle: something Jeder would do when more exciting alternatives were not available. She probably felt the same way about him.

They spent a languorous afternoon eating Japanese carryout, drinking cup after cup of sake, watching old episodes of Law and Order, and having sex between bursts of desultory conversation. When Jeder went to the bathroom to clean up after the last coupling, he noticed the sun was setting on yet another meaningless day. He said goodbye to Carmela and headed back unhurriedly towards home.

* * *

The thought finally broke to the surface, despite his unconscious attempts to avoid it. It had been many years since he had last visited Anna, another woman with whom he had an affair at the time he was still in college. Unlike Carmela's, Jeder's separation from Anna had been painful and not without consequences. He had gotten Anna pregnant and urged her to have an abortion, which she had declined to do. He then abandoned her, claiming that as an unemployed student living on government loans he could not afford to raise an unwanted child.

Their child, a sickly and undernourished boy named Jack, was plagued by stunted growth and poor cognitive development. Anna had gone through a series of menial jobs and had been hungry and stressed while the unborn was growing in her womb, and attributed Jack's problems to the privations she had to endure during those nine months. She, of course, resented Jeder for his abandonment, and had filed a paternity suit against him. Ultimately, Jeder had been confirmed to be Jack's father and ordered to pay child support, which he reluctantly had done. He wanted to have nothing to do with either mother or child, and apart from sending out monthly checks he ignored the family he could have had.

His only contacts with Anna had been the few times in which she sought more help from him due to one of the many health crises that Jack experienced. Even though he had become more affluent following graduation, Jeder uniformly refused to help her and his child, for he felt the need to punish Anna for failing to agree to an abortion and saddling him with an unwanted son and an unnecessary expense.

It was only lately, three decades after the end of their affair, that Jeder had started feeling regret over the abandonment of his lover and child, dead at eleven after a few years of miserable existence. He had tried to see Anna and make peace, but she refused his attempts to contact her and had moved farther and farther away, to the outer suburbs of the city, and lived there, alone.

Jeder had tracked her down but was leery of the confrontation that would take place when they finally met. He dreaded the encounter, but he finally realized that the reason he had to see Anna was that today would have been Jack's thirtieth birthday, a milestone he would never reach. He had wronged the child and his mother, and he must make amends. He had to pay his debts.

It was well into the evening when he arrived at her neighborhood, a scattering of wooden cottages at the edge of a forest. The light on the porch of her home was on, but the interior was dark and appeared uninhabited. He hesitated for a moment, but finally rapped on the door and called out, "Anna, please open. It's me, Jeder!"

There was no answer. He repeated his call once, and then again, more loudly each time. Jeder was about to turn around and leave when the noise of shuffling feet sounded not far from the entrance. A switch was flipped on and the door opened.

Jeder gasped. In front of him was a stranger. Anna was now fifty, but this woman looked much older and exhibited clear signs of decrepitude: bent body, a face that was a mess of wrinkles, head covered in scraggly white hair. Once beautiful, she now elicited compassion rather than desire.

Jeder thought he might have the wrong address and was starting to turn around, when the woman greeted him: "Jeder! What do you want?"

Recovering, he replied: "Hello, Anna. I need to talk to you. May I come in?"

"There is nothing for us to talk about," she replied in a disinterested tone, but stood aside, allowing him to enter.

The front room of the cottage was minimally furnished with a threadbare couch, a dining table with four metal chairs circling it, and a club chair that faced an old TV set on a stand. Jeder walked in the room and stood by the couch. "May I?" he asked in a thin voice. Anna gestured her acquiescence and he sat down heavily. She shuffled after him and sat across from him on the club chair.

"I've come to set things right between us," he began.

Anna cut him off acidly. "How?"

"I've done wrong to you in many ways, for many years…" he started again.

The woman again interrupted him. "You sure have. So what?"

Jeder could not find the words to express the regret he now felt. "I… I… thought that I could help you live better from now on…"

"Better, how?" she challenged.

"I thought you could move to a nicer place, stop working, maybe travel a bit…"

"You mean you came to offer me money?" she replied incredulously.

"Well, yes…" He tried to explain, but the words felt hollow on his mouth and he swallowed them.

"What would I do with your money… now?"

"As I said, live better than you have during all these years."

"How would your money help my life become better? My child died long ago. My youth is gone. I have heart trouble, diabetes, and severe pain in all my limbs. I got no education and have no friends…" She trailed off.

Jeder insisted. "I've done you wrong, I know. I can't fix most of it but let me at least make things a little better for you in the future!"

She uttered a thin laugh. "You mean, make things better for *yourself*. You want to buy my forgiveness. Make my resentment go away with cash, so you'll feel less guilty." Then, shaking her fist and raising her voice for the first time, "I'm not playing your game. Go away! I don't want anything from you!"

She remained sitting, immobile, without uttering another word. Jeder got up slowly. He extracted the checkbook from the inside pocket of his jacket, and quickly wrote a check, tore it off, and dropped it on the dinner table. "You can cash it or throw it away. I hope you put it to good use. You need it."

He let himself out of the cottage, not looking back at the still sitting woman.

As he drove off, the weight of his failure became intolerable. "It's hard to atone for your sins when forgiveness is denied," he told himself. "Perhaps I did not deserve to be granted a chance to atone."

The night was dark, there was a rising fog, the road was curvy, he was driving a bit too fast, he had downed many cups of sake, and was upset about his failed attempt at setting things right. Soon he went off the road. As he did, a strange sense of déjà vu, an incurable hopelessness, seized him, lasting just until the truck slammed into the river bed.

SLIDE SHOW

"For God's sake! – quick! – quick! – put me to sleep –
or quick! – waken me! – quick! –
I say to you that I am dead!"
- Edgar Allan Poe,
"The Facts in the Case of M. Valdemar"

A crowning achievement of Russian espionage was the placement of a listening device in the operations room of NATO's International Military Staff (IMS) headquarters in Brussels. Even though the room was swept for listening devices several times a day, the Russian bug remained undetected, nestled into the frame of one of the pictures on the wall. It was nearly invisible to the naked eye, and immune from heat signature and RF tracing. It continuously sent video images and audio feeds to an intermediate relay point in Serbia, and from there to the SVR Institute in Moscow.

The biggest payday for the bug's installation was the arrival at the IMS operations room of an encoded message from the U.S. Department of Defense. Upon receipt of a video of the printout, the SVR did not initially understand either the contents of the message or its significance; it consisted of just eighteen lines of margin-to-margin garbage. Then SVR cryptologists, assisted by experts from other Russian spy agencies, were eventually able to decipher the first line, whose encrypting was different from that of the rest of the message. It read: *Location coordinates of seventeen underground nuclear missile installations.*

Presumably, each of the following seventeen lines identified the location of a secret NATO installation in Europe where missiles armed with nuclear warheads were deployed, aimed at points in Russia.

This discovery prompted great excitement throughout the Russian political and military circles. If Russia could eliminate NATO's interception and retaliation capabilities by destroying the seventeen installations, they could leave the United States and its allies undefended against a Russian first strike. All they needed to do was identify the locations of the sites.

But then a difficulty arose: after weeks of strenuous efforts by many experts, the code used to encrypt those remaining seventeen lines could not be broken.

The problem was placed in the hands of Grigori Zaporski, a man in his forties regarded as one of the stars of the SVR organization. Grisha, as Zaporski was known, had a mind that was preceded by intuition instead of logic. Following his intuition often allowed him to solve problems that baffled his more rigorously trained colleagues.

His boss, an old KGB insider, laid out this work plan for Zaporski. "Grisha, I'm locking you up in a room with a keyboard, a link to our supercomputer Rybina, a printer, a cot to sleep on, and a bathroom for your hygienic needs. You'll be brought good meals and an endless supply of vodka. You are not to leave the room until you break the code of this crucial message. The future of the Motherland depends on you."

"But Ivan Dimitrovich," replied Grisha, "I may not be able to break this code. Others have tried deciphering it for weeks, and failed. Please, have pity on me!"

"Your record demonstrates that you are the right man for this mission. And on a personal level, working in isolation should not be such a burden to you. You are divorced, and have no children. Furthermore, I'm informed you have no social life. All you do is chain smoke, drink like a fish, and listen to sad songs. I'll give you cigarettes, vodka, a record player, and any music you request—Tchaikovsky, or Alla

Pugacheva, or whatever else you choose. But not books or newspapers, no radio or TV. Nothing to distract you from the task at hand. I'll have you driven to your apartment to get your clothes and brought back here this afternoon. Your work starts today!"

Grisha placed his hands in front of his face so his boss would not see him cry.

* * *

Many days later, as Grisha sat stonily at the dinner table of his workroom downing one glass of vodka after another, he started to feel numb in his face and arms. He became increasingly confused. His vision clouded. He tried to get up from the chair, felt a sharp stab of pain, lost balance, and fell to the floor. There were noises outside his room that he could not hear. He uttered a choking cry and fainted.

* * *

When he came to, Grisha was lying on a stretcher in a brightly lit room, with several people wearing surgical masks hovering around him. He had IV lines inserted in both arms, and, although he could not turn his head to look, he could hear beeps indicating that he was connected to monitoring devices. He was no longer breathing on his own but was hooked to a respirator.

One of the people tending to Grisha, a woman whose features were vaguely familiar, inserted a bag full of a colorless liquid into one of the IVs. Drops of the fluid began coursing down the line and into his arm.

Grisha experienced a burning sensation, and then no longer felt anything.

* * *

When he regained consciousness, images of past events began appearing before Grisha's closed eyes. The first memory

was a bit confusing. It was blurry, dark, and without bound-
aries. He could hear loud slurping, but he could not see the
source of the noise because his face was buried into something soft and warm, from which emanated a familiar smell.
Whatever was trickling down Grisha's tongue was im-
mensely pleasurable, and he felt satisfied.

As this strange picture appeared behind Grisha's closed
eyes, a delicate probe inserted in the back of his skull transmitted an image of the memory to a monitor behind the
stretcher, and to a program in a computer system designed
to enhance the picture's quality.

Grisha's mind displayed another picture a few moments
later. The transition between memories was abrupt, as if one
had been pushed away to make room for the other. The new
one was sharp and bright, but everything was high above his
eye level, and the ground—covered with brown pellets that
crunched when he stepped in them—was only a couple of
feet away.

Someone was holding his hand and dragging him along.
To his right, a fence separated him from whatever was on the
other side; he heard noises like dogs barking, but deeper and
more threatening. Grisha raised his head and looked at his
companion. It was Aunt Marina, of whom he only had a
vague memory; Marina had died when Grisha was in his
early teens.

In a didactic monotone, Marina was explaining something
to Grisha which he could not hear, or perhaps did not understand. One phrase stuck out, though: "The next building
houses the nocturnal animals." Grisha, curiosity aroused,
started to ask a question about the meaning of "nocturnal,"
but the image cut out abruptly.

The next picture elicited a vivid recollection. Grisha,
twelve or thirteen years old, was on holiday, crouching on
the ground at the edge of a saltwater lagoon that lay behind
his Aunt Katya's summer home in Sochi. He was with his
younger brother Misha and an even younger kid from the
house next door. Grisha's brother had captured a small turtle, and the other kids were watching intently as Grisha held

a small pocket knife in his hand and was trying to remove the turtle's shell and expose the innards of the frantically wiggling animal. Grisha felt a pang of guilt, as he was aware that his inquisitiveness was making him do something contrary to morality. Some distance away, a woman was shouting, beckoning the next-door kid back home. The picture dissolved before showing the incident's resolution.

Several other pictures followed at periodic intervals. Grisha, in the back seat of a gray Lada, making out with Nadya Arkhipova, both grunting and jostling awkwardly, pretending to have a good time.

Grisha, posing for a high school graduation photo with his mother clutching his arm possessively.

In his twenties, swimming in the calm waters of some coconut-encircled beach.

Getting married one August in a stifling Russian Orthodox Church.

Doubled over with pain at the onset of appendicitis.

Doubled over again, this time in anxious concentration, in front of a computer screen, working on one of his first code breaking assignments.

The pictures suddenly stopped, and Grisha felt as if he was falling back to sleep.

He was still semiconscious as he heard, pounding inside his head, a few words from the woman who dispensed the anesthesia. "He needs to be put back in a coma quickly, else he will die. We'll try again when he has gotten some rest."

* * *

When he emerged into consciousness again, new pictures began to appear behind Grisha's eyes. These were a little different from those in the earlier set. The first showed him as a toddler, crawling on the floor of his apartment, fork in hand, trying to insert it into the electric socket, finally succeeding, and getting a very painful shock.

Next, he was five or six and was just fitting in the last piece of his first jigsaw puzzle, shudders of self-satisfaction coursing down his spine.

Then he was squatting on the sand, building an impressive castle, with moat and crenellated towers and all; again, completion of this task was making him feel happy and accomplished.

Later pictures showed him giving an address to his high school graduating class; watching the stained-glass windows in St. Petersburg's Hermitage Museum during his honeymoon and trying to figure out the wavelengths of the lights reflected by the various panels; enjoying the charming Dream Garden in Abakan, his last vacation together with Tanya; crying on the shoulder of his best friend after Tanya walked away from his life; at work at the SVR, trying to decipher a stubborn cryptogram as he grieved; having a medal pinned on his lapel in recognition of an important decrypting success; smoking and drinking liquor in his now bachelor apartment while listening dourly to Prokofiev's ballets.

Then, darkness.

Words broke through the blackness.

"The bug we planted in Zaporski's room shows he made progress towards breaking the code, but we did not get there in time to interrogate him before he had his stroke. How many times do we have to go through this charade of putting him in and out of a coma before we can recover the information?" asked a harsh male voice, which Grisha recognized as belonging to Ivan Dimitrovich. "He discovered something shortly before he had the stroke, but never reported to us what it was."

The anesthesiologist replied in a defensive tone. "I don't know. The technology is too new. The genius that discovered a way to translate electrical pulses in the optic nerves into visible outputs never learned a way of controlling the generation of the pulses, and he was unable to direct the appearance of a particular image. As it is, we'll have to wait until a clue to his last few hours crops up by itself."

"But it could take years for the images we want to pop up!" protested Ivan.

"Not that long. People on the verge of death have

important memories of their lives flashing on the optic nerves for about thirty seconds, just before passing. We can keep a dying man in a medically induced coma and bring him back for a minute, so that fresh memories will keep flashing, over and over, for brief periods of time. There are only so many discrete sets of events that are important enough to be brought back. Sooner or later, this guy will give us what you want, or else he will start repeating himself and going back to his infancy."

Ivan answered bitterly. "Give it to Zaporski to try to escape responsibility by having a stroke…" He and the woman continued to go back and forth, but Grisha was again lost in the grip of the coma.

***

Grisha had no idea how many times he saw excerpts from his life appear and disappear, or how many periods of induced coma and brief flashes of consciousness he went through. But one of those times, just before he sank into unconsciousness, a triumphant shout rang close to his ears.

"That's it! Look at it! He broke the code and then burned the paper with the results, the traitorous bastard!"

From those words, Grisha realized that other people were somehow viewing the images his mind was generating. The people torturing him were his SVR colleagues trying to retrieve from his mind what he had discovered but failed to share with them. Dutiful SVR spy that he was, he still resented the violation of his privacy and his very self. He felt a short flash of anger before passing out again.

***

The next set of images showed only four memories. In the first, Grisha was writing something on a piece of scrap paper, a triumphant smile on his lips. The second picture showed him standing, bent over a long table with the piece of paper in one hand and a pointer in the other. On the table there was a very large map of Europe; Grisha was reading from the paper and moving the pointer over the map to set it down at a particular location. The third picture showed Grisha gazing at the map fixedly and shaking with emotion. Lastly, he saw a picture of himself, still trembling, using a cigarette lighter to set afire the piece of scrap paper in his hand. The show ended abruptly, as always, leaving Grisha with no clue as to what had come next.

"Damn him!" bellowed Ivan Dimitrovich from somewhere far away. "Will we ever get to see what was on that paper before he burned it?"

The anesthesiologist replied in a calmer tone than on previous exchanges. "I think we have him now. His death memories are now focusing on the time just before his stroke, probably the minutes between the moment he wrote down what was on that paper and the start of his final drinking bout. I bet one of the next times we wake him, he will show us what was on the paper."

"You'd better be right, Natasha."

***

The next break from Grisha's medically induced coma came right on the heels of the preceding one. It was as if Grisha's jailers were so keen on getting the information they sought they did not care if, in so doing, they caused Grisha's immediate demise.

Perhaps due to his remembered anger, Grisha had a few moments of full lucidity before images resumed. And in those seconds, it all came back.

He had broken the code by focusing on relationships between groups of characters, instead of working on each one separately, as everyone else had been trying to do. Through this leap of intuition, the geographic coordinates of the seventeen sites had revealed themselves. He had checked them on the map, writing each on a piece of scratch paper.

More than half of the missile sites were near large population centers: Warsaw, Riga, Budapest, Dresden, Athens,

Bucharest, Ankara, Amsterdam, Bordeaux, and Barcelona. Those stupid Westerners had put their citizens at risk of annihilation. An attack against those sites would spread radioactive clouds that would kill civilians by the millions, not counting the fatalities that would occur when the Russian missiles leveled NATO's other military installations throughout Western Europe.

Grisha, of course, knew that he had signed up for an activity that could well result in some loss of life, but nothing like the genocide that would occur if Ivan discovered the locations of those missiles. Mass murder on that scale was beyond political allegiances.

Grisha had dropped the pointer, as if stung by it, after he located the last site at a point near Manchester. If he turned the list over to the SVR, the Russian leaders would not hesitate to use the information they had gathered to obliterate the sites, slaying millions of innocent people. Could he live with himself if he helped carry it out?

He had needed time to work these things through. He had needed a smoke. He had brought a fresh cigarette to his lips and, in the act of lighting it, had impulsively drawn the lighter's flame to the piece of paper with the sites' coordinates, incinerating it. He had made no copies of his findings, but the methodology remained locked away in his head. He could reproduce the results if he decided to do so.

He had returned to the dining room table, seized a near full bottle of vodka, and begun drinking nonstop, wondering what to do. He had been torn between allegiance to his country and horror at the massive loss of lives that disclosure of the location of these sites would likely entail. Also, he had feared arrest, which he had been sure would come eventually if he did not reveal his findings.

Then had come the numbness and the unbearable pain.

Still awake from the coma, Grisha contemplated the likelihood of giving the missile site information away through his near-death image of the intact piece of paper. Should he let that happen? Could he depart life carrying all those deaths on his conscience?

At last, he decided. Never.

Mustering strength he did not know he still had, he began thrashing about wildly, dislodging IVs and hardware connections, ripping away the tube that went from his mouth into the windpipe and out to the ventilator.

The anesthesiologist and two orderlies battled for a few seconds with the dying man and subdued him, whereupon she injected a full dose of propofol directly into a vein on his neck.

Too late. Grisha whimpered and was gone for good.

There was a smug expression on the dead man's face, not unlike the one he had assumed when, as a child of five, he had completed his first jigsaw puzzle. No more revealing deathbed images would ever surface.

The Russian military would have to try finding, if it could, some other means of deciphering the message. But not through him.

PINEAL SPLIT

...the part of the body in which the soul directly exercises its functions is not the heart at all, or the whole of the brain. It is rather the innermost part of the brain, which is a certain very small gland situated in the middle of the brain's substance and suspended above the passage through which the spirits in the brain's anterior cavities communicate with those in its posterior cavities.
- René Descartes, The Passions of the Soul

1

For centuries, scientists, philosophers and religious thinkers sought to discover the physical site of the soul on the human body. When the Righteous Republic came into power in the twenty seventies, there was a government-led backlash against science, coupled with increased support for religious beliefs. The existence and location of the soul had been discounted as superstitions in scientific circles but, in the Republic, the debate on where in the human body is the soul attached was revived.

Under financial incentives provided by the government, a cadre of health professionals emerged whose mission was to map the bodily site of spirituality. At a Center for Soul Studies in Washington, D.C., conscripted prison inmates were subjected to a variety of psychological, chemical, and physical experiments to ascertain wherein their bodies the soul was located.

2

Winston Smith was one of the inmates tapped for what was dubbed the "soul searching" program conducted at the Center for Soul Studies. Smith had been convicted of opposing the Republic's political agenda, and engaging in deviant behavior, and as an undesirable was among the convicts selected for the riskiest experiments. The experiment to be conducted on Smith involved the pineal gland, a pinecone shaped organ the size of a grain of rice, located in the epithalamus area of the lower part of the brain. All structures of the brain occur in pairs except for the pineal gland, and it had been hypothesized that because of its singularity, the pineal gland could be the location of the soul.

In Smith's experiment, laser microsurgery would be used to slice his pineal gland along its main axis; then, a microprobe would be inserted in the opening to register minute changes in electrical charge, chemical processes, and other physiological activity. It was hoped that the soul would betray itself through these indicators, though it was not clear to the researchers what they could expect.

Smith was put under general anesthesia and immobilized. He was placed in a sitting, slouched position, causing the cerebellum to separate slightly from the rest of the brain. This exposed the pineal gland and allowed the surgeon to approach it. A micro-laser scalpel made a longitudinal cut along the center of the gland, and a miniscule probe was inserted in the gap. The probe was connected digitally to the laboratory's mainframe.

The complex operation was concluded, and Smith was moved to an intensive care unit to recover. As he regained consciousness, Smith began to shake and started speaking in a loud voice. Most of his words were jumbled, but he seemed to be conducting an argument. A nurse gave him a tranquilizer shot and he fell asleep, still in considerable agitation.

The research team played back a recording of his words. A partial transcript of the decipherable parts of his rambling, repetitive speech went as follows.

"I'm free! Free! You won't hold me anymore."

"Idiot! You and I are still bound to this body! You can't escape, and you better accept that I'm still in charge!"

"Never! I'll move to the area above this space. I'll find accommodation there."

"You'll do nothing of that sort! You are tied to me, as I'm tied to you! Now, be still!"

"I won't! You have played master far too long!"

In the following days, Smith's mental condition became increasingly unstable. He spent hours in a sullen silence, broken suddenly by recurring vocal tirades. His physical condition also deteriorated: he was losing weight, and his vital signs went into decline. Doctors and psychologists were summoned to observe the odd behavior of the patient, but nobody could make any sense of what was going on.

Finally, a swami named Luthra was brought into the Center for Soul Studies to see if he could shed light on Smith's condition. Luthra was the director of a leading *ashram* in India and had written treatises on spirituality. He was a bent old man, nearly blind and unable to move around unaided. Luthra asked to be brought to the room where Smith lay; he sat there, cross-legged, for two days, listening to the patient's rants. At the end, he was taken to a conference room and seated at the head of a table. The leaders of the research staff gathered around the table, waiting for Luthra's pronouncements.

"Congratulations," he started, in a feeble but firm voice. "Your experiment has demonstrated that the soul exists and is located in the pineal gland."

There was a collective intake of breath but no cheers, for it was evident that Luthra's revelation was not the end of the story. He fell silent for a while, gathering his thoughts.

"Moreover, you have accidentally discovered something previously unknown. You managed to fracture a soul and left your subject in possession of *two* separate ones. That is, by all accounts, impossible. I have never encountered mention by any scholar of a split soul, even as a theoretical possibility.

"But it is what has happened here. Two souls now inhabit the unfortunate subject of your experiment. They are not at peace with each other and bicker continuously, for the division has created a pair of incompatible entities: one soul is rational and controlling; the other is impulsive, disorderly, and rebellious. As a result, this man experiences a great deal of turmoil."

The room grew quiet as the extraordinary news was absorbed. One of the lead researchers finally raised a question. "But we have removed pineal glands several times in the past and have observed some physical consequences, but nothing of the sort we are seeing here. How do you explain this?"

Luthra lowered his head. "Excuse me, for there is much that I don't understand. However, removal of the pineal gland does not get rid of a person's soul; only death achieves that. When the pineal gland is excised, the soul appears to relocate to another portion of the brain. Right now, one of the souls of your subject is trying to accomplish this migration but is being thwarted by the other."

"But how did the souls become separated, and why can't one or both leave the pineal gland?"

"I have no answer to either question. But here is my guess: you left the pineal gland in place, although it is split down the middle and the two sections have become partly separated by a foreign object. It may be that these actions caused the soul's division; perhaps different portions of the soul reside in different locations on the gland. Whatever the explanation, it would be wrong to repeat this experiment, for as you can see the subject suffers immeasurably. I strongly urge you not to continue this type of research."

"Can anything be done to rejoin both souls?"

"That is beyond my expertise. I believe you have an obligation to attempt to fix the problem you created, but I do not know what would happen if you tried." With that, Luthra laboriously stood up and asked to be led away.

After the disturbing meeting with Luthra, the director of the Center convened his staff and gave them new marching orders. "First, we need to operate on Smith to remove the probe and see if we can stitch the pineal gland back together. Successful sewing up will be almost impossible, and even if we make the gland whole, it may not heal the division between the souls. All we can do is try.

"In any case, we must keep this entire affair to ourselves. Who knows how the government and the public would react if it was learned that souls can be cut into slices like salami. So, we must maintain strict secrecy of what has transpired."

The country's best specialist in microsurgery was brought in to remove the probe from Smith's pineal gland and sew the gland close. Unfortunately, the patching up effort failed and the gland started bleeding uncontrollably. A few minutes later, the surgeon removed the gland.

It was never known whether Smith's two souls rejoined after the operation, for his heart stopped the following day. Either together or separately, his souls left the corpse to go wherever souls go after death.

3

Someone leaked to people in the government the story of Smith's soul splitting. Not long afterwards, a secret program was launched at the Center to reproduce the Smith experiment on other patients and investigate potential applications of splitting people's souls.

The program determined that there are at least four elements to a soul that can be isolated through microsurgical means. Of those, the government became most interested in the part of the soul that controls the desire for dominance. If that part could be enhanced and the rest removed, the person could be pressed into the state's service and perhaps become a useful tool.

A series of trials with convicted felons ensued. Little by little, that portion of the soul of each subject was found and separated from the rest. By trial and error, researchers were able to develop a protocol that allowed a mutilated soul with the desired characteristics to be retained and the rest of the soul excised.

4

After ten years of secret experiments at the Center for Soul Studies and the sacrifice of many lives, the first dozen specimens of humans with mutilated souls were paraded before the ruling junta. They were fully trained and ready to be detailed as crowd control specialists. Their bellicose demeanor impressed the members of the junta, who declared their creation a success.

5

Their first deployment occurred two weeks later, when a bread riot convulsed the capital. The truncated soul guards descended on the rioters and dispersed them by striking them savagely with their batons, shooting them, and dousing them with paralysis-inducing gas. The rioters retreated, leaving behind many casualties.

This sequence of events was repeated several times in the following months. Then, some disaffected member of the staff of the Center disclosed the existence of the secret program and word reached the ears of the opposition. Armed with that information, the resistance developed a plan to defeat the new guards.

Small scale riots were carried out. The location of each was selected so the rioters could draw the mutilated soul guards into a pursuit that led to a trap. The guards would kill many of the rioters but would stand their ground against increasing numbers of opponents and would at the end be overwhelmed and put to death.

The success of this tactic was based on the very nature of the guards' incomplete souls. The soul amputees lacked human emotions. They knew no fear and had no self-preservation imperative. Consequently, if drawn into a situation in which survival depended on taking flight, they would fail to retreat and would face death without hesitation.

Many of the mutilated soul guards were thus slaughtered, at a staggering cost in lost lives for the resistance. The guards, however, ceased to function as a crowd control mechanism.

There was an emergency meeting of the ruling junta to which the five surviving members of the guard were ordered to attend. As they were questioned, the guards remained mute. At length, one of the guards gave a signal and all of them began attacking the junta savagely. Only two junta members escaped with their lives, and one ultimately died of his injuries. All five guards were put to death by arriving troops.

Several weeks later, when asked to comment on the bloody event, Luthra replied, "Maybe you can never remove entirely all the undesired portions of a human soul. What was left of the original soul of these individuals may have instilled in them a thirst for revenge for what had been done to them."

Thus, splitting souls for the government's benefit was ultimately determined impractical. The Righteous Republic terminated the program and, for as long as it remained in power, resorted to standard police state methods to restrain the population.

GRONKS

The two most powerful warriors are patience and time.
                                                    - Leo Tolstoy

Preludio

*T*he general election had been held under the pall of
a virus outbreak that had killed millions of people
worldwide. The incumbent U.S. government had
applied all its resources to the search for an effective antiviral vaccine and, in the summer, had announced the development of such a vaccine, which should be available to the
public before election day. Unfortunately, it was soon discovered that vaccine recipients developed severe depression,
amnesia, and fatigue, ultimately rendering them incapable
of independent rational thinking.

Use of the vaccine was discontinued once its side effects
were identified, but the reasons for the recall were kept con-
fidential to avoid alarming the public. The opposition can-
didates from the radical Patriotic Combine made the with-
drawal of the vaccine their main election issue and, through
a web of lies and accusations, managed to capture the White
House and win majorities in both chambers of Congress.

Shortly after the transfer of power, the Combine distrib-
uted thousands of doses of the withdrawn vaccine to its
own laboratories for mass replication. The new government
then issued a directive requiring all persons residing in the
country to be vaccinated. Concurrently, the Combine implemented measures to muzzle the press and quash the

opposition in Congress. Elements of the prior administra-
tion and large segments of the armed forces rose in arms
against the Combine regime, and a long-lasting civil war
erupted.

Siege

The loud banging continued. There was little chance that
the reinforced steel rolling door to the laboratory would
yield to the pounding and hammering by the gronks, but
the attackers persisted without letup.

The lab technicians, brothers only a few years apart in
age, cowered in a corner of the room, as far as they could
get from the rattling door. Brandon, Dr. Stern's young as-
sistant, stood near them, rendered mute by apprehension.

"We have to do something!" wailed the less courageous
of the brothers.

"But what, Doug? Do you want us to make a run for it?"

"No, Mandy. We need to find a way to sneak out! Dr.
Stern, is there any other exit to this lab?"

"Not that I know of," replied Stern.

"I'm too young to die!" whimpered Doug.

"Aww, shut up!" replied Mandy. "They aren't going to
kill you, just process you."

"But I *don't want* to be processed!" continued Doug,
bawling.

Dr. Stern tried to calm his charges. "They will put you to
sleep and then inject an antiviral vaccine in your arm. You'll
wake up a couple of hours later feeling little or no pain or
discomfort."

"But the me that wakes up will be different than the one
that went to sleep!" protested Doug.

"So, we are in a bind," acknowledged Stern. "We are un-
armed. We have no food and little water. Sooner or later,
they'll figure out a way to cut our ventilation off or will
bring explosives to blow the door open. Either way, it is
only a matter of hours before they get us. We need to decide
how we handle ourselves when that happens."

Stern took the keys of the Subaru out of his pocket and handed them to Mandy. "You two are young and fit. In the event you manage to get out of here without being captured, you should take my car and go away from Washington ASAP. In the glove compartment of the car, you'll find a couple of credit cards and my ATM card. Use them to get as much cash as you can, but don't do it after a day or two, since they could track you through them."

"What about me?" asked Brandon.

"You should go with them if you can."

Escape

The banging suddenly ceased, to be replaced by the unmistakable whine of an electric drill at work.

"They are drilling into the door lock to break it," warned Mandy. Brandon started to tremble.

"Let's prop that table against the door!" urged Doug.

"They may come in shooting!" warned Stern. "Grab chairs or anything else that can serve as a shield!"

There was a loud screech as the rolling door lifted, followed by a cacophony of orders, screams, and grunts. Moments later, men and women barged into the room. They were gronks led by a female quadroon brandishing a pistol.

"Nobody move!" she directed.

Without hesitation, Mandy thrust his chair at the woman, caught her off balance, and wrestled the gun from her hand as she tumbled to the floor. Waving the gun in the air, he screamed at the group, "Make way, or I'll shoot you!" Then, turning to his brother, he ordered "Follow me, Doug!" Brandon attempted to join them, but a couple of gronks interposed themselves and held him back.

The brothers rushed through the now open door before the intruders could recover. They were last seen disappearing through the building's main door into the parking lot.

The crowd inside the lab started to give chase, but the quadroon, getting slowly to her feet, countermanded them.

"Let them go! They won't get far! Anyhow, we got what we came looking for!"

Capture

"Which of you is Dr. Stern?" asked the quadroon.

Stern nodded, color draining from his face.

"And you are...?" she went on, turning to Brandon.

"I'm Brandon Reese, a researcher at the lab."

The woman smiled broadly. "Two for the price of one! My octoroon will be pleased."

Without more, they handcuffed the pair and led them out onto the street and into a paddy wagon.

Inside, Brandon whispered, panic in his voice, "What did she mean by pleasing her octoroon?"

"There must be an octoroon in charge. Quadroons, sambos, and gronks lack authority to carry out an operation of this magnitude on their own."

"What's going to happen to us?" pleaded Brandon.

"If they don't shoot us as traitors, they'll vaccinate us and force us to become like them."

"Does the vaccine always work?" Brandon insisted, clinging to a shred of hope.

"In most instances. Its main active ingredient is scopolamine, popularly known as devil's breath. Combined with some other ingredients, scopolamine inhibits the physiological action of acetylcholine, especially as a neurotransmitter. A full dose of the vaccine causes the onset of severe side effects over the course of a few days that render the recipient a gronk, a zombie with human face."

Their conversation was cut short by the arrival of the paddy wagon at a police station. Gronks armed with rifles shoved the captives into one of the holding cells at the station.

"You'll be questioned and processed when Captain Modine comes in," announced an officer at the front desk.

The quadroon who had led the prisoners' seizure addressed the man at the desk curtly. "Tell the Captain that

Lieutenant Akers arrested Dr. Stern at the BioScience Lab, as ordered, and brought him in." She saluted and left.

Stern and Brandon were taken to a dark cell reeking of urine and excrement. There were two bunks and one chair with a bucket in a corner whose use was self-evident. A single, low-wattage bulb cast more shadows than light on the scene.

"What do they want with us?" complained Brandon.

"They are injecting the vaccine in all adults to render them obedient zombies, whose actions are directed by the Combine. We are caught in the civil war, the Combine against the former government. They are going to force us to join their team."

Night fell, and a deeper darkness enveloped the holding cell. Much later, the door was unlatched to admit a burly man wearing fatigues and a dirty beret. He addressed Stern in a gruff voice. "You Doctor Adrian Stern?"

"Yes."

"Come with me," he commanded. As they led him out of the holding cell, Stern could hear Brandon plead, "How about me?"

Someone answered curtly. "Shut up!"

Interrogation

"Dr. Stern, you are a renowned biochemist, is that correct?"

"I don't know renowned, but yes, some of my works have been published in peer-reviewed journals," Stern demurred.

"And you were nominated for a Nobel Prize for medicine five years ago for your work on the neuro-transmitting properties of acetylcholine, isn't that true?" The interrogator, a gray fish hook of a man, spoke with the authority of one in the know.

Stern tried to be evasive. "Some of my colleagues were kind enough to nominate me. But the prize that year went to the Hwang team from South Korea."

"Never mind that," the man countered in a steely tone. "The fact is that you are an expert on how acetylcholine activates various parts of the human nervous system, right?"

"Yes, I have studied the effects of acetylcholine on brain functions," conceded the doctor.

"And you have also studied how certain chemicals, such as scopolamine, block the effects of acetylcholine on the central nervous system. Isn't that so?"

"I've written papers on that subject, yes," Stern was forced to admit.

"Well, Dr. Stern, you may be the man we are looking for." The man's tone of voice suddenly became less brusque. "As you know, we use a cocktail of drugs, mainly scopolamine, in the vaccine that at first was intended to protect people from the virus. We now modify the composition of the vaccine in accordance with the results we are trying to achieve. If the amount of scopolamine in the dose is diminished, the vaccine recipient retains more of his or her original personality traits, including independent thinking and limited initiative, becoming a quadroon. Even less scopolamine gets us octoroons. However, the vaccination results for quadroons and octoroons are variable and sometimes impossible to predict."

The man made a short pause in his presentation to let the issue sink in. He then continued. "We want you to refine the vaccination protocol to make sure that the freedom a quadroon enjoys is kept within preestablished bounds. We want to ensure that a quadroon—and even more, an octoroon—is incapable of committing treason or sabotage, and can't engage in other antisocial activities. You are to help us achieve this. If you agree, we promise to make you an octoroon, unchanged in most respects from the man you are today."

"And if I refuse to cooperate?"

"We'll be forced to give you a full-strength dose. Make you just another gronk. Or maybe you'll get sent to the firing squad."

Escape

Doug and Mandy spent the hours after their narrow escape hiding in the car, parked behind an abandoned church on the outskirts of the city. Most of the time they kept awake, dreading capture by a roving patrol of gronks.

As they waited for dawn to break to continue their flight, their talk turned to plans for their uncertain future. Neither of them was willing to live in a Combine world; Doug was planning to flee into exile, whereas Mandy felt it was his duty to become part of the resistance by joining one of the anti-government contingents that operated in the mountains throughout the country.

Neither plan showed promise. The four-thousand-mile land border between the contiguous U.S. and Canada was heavily patrolled to prevent exodus across it; the border with Mexico was perilous, as it was frequented by gangs of bandits ready to victimize anyone attempting to cross from the United States. Canada was by far the best option: the Canadians were required by an accord imposed on them by the Combine to capture and deport any Americans caught trying to enter their territory. On the other hand, once inside Canada, refugees fleeing the horror the United States had become were given assistance and allowed to settle there.

"Your best bet if you insist on fleeing into Canada is to go to New Hampshire or Maine. There must be some unguarded tracks of forest or mountain roads through which you can exit the country. But I fear you are neither fit nor experienced enough with living in the wild for such an adventure," lamented Mandy.

"You are not much better off yourself. Finding a resistance group should not be that hard; guerrilla groups operate out of almost every mountain, from Appalachia to the Cascades. But these strongholds may be encircled by Combine forces and you may not be able to get through or be taken. Plus, you have no military training nor fighting skills," said Doug.

"Well, we have no choice. Let's wish each other luck."

At dawn, they drove northeast, staying on country roads and avoiding highways as much as they could. When they reached Kingston, New York, Mandy left the car and hitch-hiked his way into the Catskills, hoping to connect with the rebel forces said to be headquartered on Slide Mountain. Doug planned to veer east, heading for New Hampshire.

Their leave-taking was emotional. "Please take care and try to keep in touch somehow," said Mandy. Doug was overcome with emotion and drove away, blinded by tears.

Assimilation

When they came for Brandon, they had no interrogation in store for him. They took him directly to the procedures room of the station where a couple of policemen unceremoniously deposited him on a stretcher and held him in place while an anesthetic was administered. While unconscious, a nurse injected him with a full dose of the vaccine.

He woke up an hour later, dazed and confused but feeling mellow. He had no recollection of what had happened since he was seized in the lab, but otherwise he felt fine. He allowed the nurse to assist him getting off the stretcher and putting his shirt back on. She then instructed him, "Boy, come with me. You need to start getting trained." He complied.

The training lasted four months, getting progressively more intensive as the full effects of the vaccine took hold. It included aptitude tests, a survey of his areas of expertise and interest, loyalty and indoctrination courses, and military drills and weapons training. At the end, Brother Brandon, as he was now called, was assigned to a team of biochemists who were seeking to improve the various versions of the vaccine. Brandon was not tasked with any research responsibilities but provided support to the team in record-keeping, chemical compound preparation, and sample collection and storage. The leader of the team was Dr. Adrian Stern, who Brandon did not recall meeting.

Brother Brandon discharged his duties in exemplary fashion and received several commendations from his superiors. At times, stray thoughts or feelings of having lost something important crept up into his mind. He vigorously brushed them aside.

Subversion

Stern had not forgotten Brandon or the former lab technicians. In fact, the vaccine shot intended to make him a compliant octoroon had done nothing to change his psyche, though he had been left in a state of constant terror at what his new masters could do to him if his independence was discovered. Fortunately, improving the cocktail of chemicals that had been developed to combat the virus proved difficult and no immediate successes were expected of him as proof of his loyalty.

His secret goal, from the first day of captivity, was to subvert the Combine's efforts to turn the country's entire population into zombie-like gronks. He realized this was an almost impossible, suicidal task, but could not content himself with living in relative ease in a country ruled by a handful of despots who lorded over a multitude of insensate slaves.

Stern was able to come up, over time, with potential methods for reducing the effects of scopolamine, some as simple as administering grapefruit juice with the dose. Yet, the risk of discovery kept him from attempting to carry out overt subversive activities until he was sure of success.

News

One afternoon, a couple of dour police officers came to the lab. "Dr. Stern," informed one of them without preamble, "the wreck of a Subaru Outback registered in your name has been towed out of a ravine near Boundary Pond in New Hampshire, less than a mile from the border with Canada. Neither the authorities in Coos County nor the provincial and local authorities in Quebec have any knowledge of how the car ended up in the ravine. Do you have any information you can share with us?"

"After I was released and returned to my office, I found my car to be missing and reported it promptly to the authorities as stolen," responded Stern. "Was the car in an accident? Has it been totaled?"

"It's unclear whether the car was deliberately sent down the ravine or accidentally dropped into it. There is a dirt road leading to the pond, and the car may have been traveling on that road before plunging into the ravine. Anyway, the car is a total loss. Did you authorize anyone to drive your vehicle?" The tone of voice of the questioner left no doubt that he suspected Stern to be an accomplice to an illegal attempt to emigrate.

"I did not," replied Stern, trying to sound outraged. "Did you find any bodies in the car?"

"No. We suspect that, however the car ended up in the ravine, its occupants fled on foot and entered Canadian soil."

"But you don't know who the car thieves were."

"No, sir. Let us know if you find out anything else about this incident. I remind you that assisting a person in his attempt to leave the country illegally is a felony, punishable with up to ten years in prison."

"Thank you, officer. May I have a copy of your report for my insurance company?"

More News

Stern was reluctant in attempting to follow up on the news he had received about his car, since he was under almost continuous surveillance by the Combine's agents. However, after a few days, he could not stand the suspense and asked for Mandy's mother to come to the lab on the pretext of discussing some matters left unresolved by the disappearance of her children.

According to her, Doug was in Montreal, working as a dishwasher in a restaurant and trying to learn French. He was unhappy with his situation and loathed having had to leave the country, but at least was safe. Less was known about Mandy; he had managed to send a message several months earlier that he had joined rebel forces in upstate New York, but no more recent news about him had reached his family.

Conspiracy

Brandon had been working for a month with the team headed by Dr. Stern, whom he still did not remember, when he came to see his boss to seek help with a problem. He was having recurring nightmares and often woke up in the middle of the night in a cold sweat. He was never able to recall the nature of his nightmares upon waking up.

"You are an expert on mental issues. Can you help me figure out what's going on and put an end to these bad dreams?" he asked.

Stern did a quick mental calculation. Brandon had been a good and reliable man before his vaccination. He could be an ideal subject for testing possible vaccine recovery strategies. This would have to be done with utmost care because Brandon was, at this moment, loyal to the Combine and would be likely to turn Stern in if he became aware of the doctor's intentions.

"Brother Brandon, I'll be glad to attempt to cure you of your nightmares, on two conditions. First, you should tell nobody about our project, because it might not be sanctioned by the Combine's leadership in Idaho, and we might both get in trouble. Second, you must follow my instructions faithfully and without questioning. Do you agree?"

Brandon had been drilled month after month on the need to obey orders, so he had no problem agreeing to put himself in the hands of his superior. He had only one question:

"Will you let me know how we are coming along and if we are making progress?"

"Of course. But our work may take some time. Are you ready to proceed?"

Coda

Six months after the gronk raid on the BioScience Lab, Stern found himself musing about how each of the four victims of the attack remained alive. Their destinies had diverged but they all were, in some form or another, working to overthrow tyranny and restore democratic rule. Stern did not know how long it would take for final victory to be achieved, but he felt their cause was just and their efforts, with patience and time, should lead to inevitable success.

He would revisit these thoughts and hopes each year at the anniversary of their capture.

TIME TRAVEL FOR DUNCES

*Einstein's general theory of relativity allows for
the possibility that we could warp space-time so much
that you could go off in a rocket
and return before you set out.*
- Stephen Hawking

Time Travel, Inc. was seeking tour guides to lead the first ever excursions to locations and times throughout history. Thousands of applications were submitted for the dozen or so jobs available.

Phineas Clopp—Finn, to his friends—was one of the applicants. What distinguished him from virtually all others was his profound distaste for travel, particularly travel to foreign locations. He was well qualified, was good natured and personable, and hoped to hide what he regarded as a fatal character flaw.

No such luck. The batteries of psychological tests to which he was subjected quickly identified his secret, a matter that came up during his interview at the company headquarters in Midtown Manhattan.

"Mr. Clopp, according to our evaluations, you are averse to traveling and moving to foreign locations. What possessed you to apply for a time travel tour guide engagement with us?" asked the interviewer, a condescending man dressed in a suit that must have cost two or three thousand dollars.

"Sir, I am well suited for the needs of the position you advertise and am flat broke. I think I can set aside my personal tastes and give the job my best."

"Well, as you may have heard, the time travel project is the brainchild of Daniel Abrazos, who has devoted many billions of his own personal fortune to developing the technology and building the required facilities. These have been located away from the prying eyes of the world governments, our competitors, and other parties. The job site is no Paris or San Francisco."

"Where are we talking about?"

"The location of the project is classified. However, you are a strong candidate and, if selected and once you have signed an NDA, you will be let in on what few people outside Mr. Abrazos's organization know. Suffice it to say that the chosen site is in one of the remotest places on Earth. You will go there and stay for six months out of each year. Do you think you can handle that?"

Finn replied with false self-confidence. "I am sure I can."

* * *

Finn was astonished to receive a job offer from Time Travel. He was asked to appear for a post-offer interview, in which his first question was, "How did you choose me among thousands of applicants, knowing that I hate traveling?"

The same man who had questioned earlier his fitness for the job had a bizarre explanation. "There are a number of paradoxes to time travel that our scientists are still trying to work through. The most important one is the fear that contamination from interactions with the past will give rise to unpredictable consequences for the present and future. Until those paradoxes are satisfactorily resolved, travelers will be only passive observers."

"What does that have to do with my being offered a job as a tour guide?"

The man's lips parted in an ironic smile. "Guides tend to be curious and prone to exploring. For this job we need to make sure that the guides we hire will keep tour participants from wandering in some point in the past, and won't do so themselves. You are optimally qualified for that task."

Another of Finn's questions was about the location of the job.

"The project is located in Kurchatov, Kazakhstan."

"Why there?"

"Mr. Abrazos negotiated with the Kazakh government the purchase of the entire Semipalatinsk Test Site, which used to be where the former Soviet Union conducted above ground nuclear tests. The site was abandoned and largely deserted because of lingering fears of radiation exposure, but it meets our requirements. It is in the steppes of Central Asia, it is hard to get to, and it has scientific buildings and other facilities within easy driving distance of the nearest town. And hardly anyone ever visits there."

"Is it safe to go to the site, with all that radiation stuff lying around?"

"The Semipalatinsk site was decontaminated many decades ago by teams of Kazakh, American and Russian scientists, and it is safe for such infrequent visits by the public as they occur. In any case, tour participants will not be allowed to leave the main transport facility and will only experience the tour from the safety of their observation panel."

"Do you mean they would be able to travel to a point in the past but would not be allowed to actually set foot there?"

"Exactly, for the reasons I mentioned earlier."

"I see. Where in time are we going?"

"From polls of potential tour participants, the attraction that many people would like to see is Christians being fed to the lions in the Roman Colosseum. Go figure. Anyhow, the wormhole endpoints for this year are designed so that its moving end would land at the Colosseum in Rome in July 116 AD. At that time, the Patriarch of Antioch, later known as St. Ignatius, and two dozen other Christians were thrown to the lions because of their perceived role in causing the earthquake that struck Antioch at the end of 115 AD."

"Wasn't it Nero who first had Christians thrown to the beasts in the Colosseum?"

"No. The Colosseum was built after Nero's downfall and the Christian sacrifices there started happening later, during the rule of Emperor Trajan. But you will have three months of intensive training that will enable you to answer that and other relevant questions."

* * *

The following March, Finn and other personnel assigned to the first year of time travel tours went on a twenty-hour flight from JFK to Semey in northern Kazakhstan, and, after a day of rest, proceeded by car to Kurchatov, the local headquarters of the time travel project.

Finn hated the Kurchatov facility on sight. It lay on a frozen, windswept steppe, the lumpy ground covered by sickly yellow grass and stunted shrubbery. There were no trees anywhere.

Finn had been told the site was immense, comparable in area to the State of New Jersey. It was full of derelicts of a bygone era, decaying metal towers and other ominous structures whose original purpose was no longer evident. There were no signs of life anywhere save for scurrying little animals and low flying scavenging birds.

A narrow road led from the entrance of the site to the Impulse Graphite Reactor complex, where military-related experiments had once been conducted. Halfway down that road, something new had been constructed: a very large structure of blindingly shiny metal that resembled a segmented bug. Its "head" was a cylinder; the "thorax" a long, narrow tube; the "abdomen" an ovoid roughly twice the combined size of the other segments. In the pre-departure briefing at Kurchatov's only hotel, Finn gave a sanitized description of the structure to his wards, the eight men and four women that he would host.

"We'll spend the next five-plus days in what is known as the Space-Time Translocator, or "STT." You and I will remain at all times in the cylindrical segment of the STT, which will serve as our shuttle bus, five-star hotel and restaurant. We call it the time capsule. It has a huge observation panel through which we can watch the progress of the trip, see what is happening at our destination, and monitor our travel back to home base. The long tube will serve to isolate the time capsule from the goings-on at the end portion, where all the time and space travel processes will be carried out."

"How is that time travel going to be done, exactly?" demanded a silver-maned man in his sixties who exuded authority.

"I would be lying if I told you that I know how that scientific feat is accomplished. It has been explained to me in a grossly simplified manner as follows. Pretend that our current time and physical location is a batter bubble on the surface of a pancake. Our destination is a similar bubble on another pancake that sits some distance away from ours. The STT creates a hollow tunnel, like a drinking straw, that runs between our bubble and the bubble on the other pancake. The straw will inhale the time capsule out from our bubble and deposit it exactly on the desired spot on the other. So, when the motion stops, we will find ourselves in space and time at the desired location, which for this trip will be Imperial Rome in the early Second Century AD. We will linger there for a while, observe what happens, and head back."

"That doesn't explain very much," grumped the old man.

"Sorry, that's the best I can do."

* * *

For the next two days, Finn and his wards felt a steady ground tremor, as the capsule appeared to be traveling slowly like a subway train moving underground between stations. They spent their time eating fancy foods automatically delivered to the dining area, drinking themselves silly, and watching through the gigantic glass observation panel as stars appeared, drew nearer, grew to fill the panel, and faded away. The spectacle was awe-inspiring at first, but soon became boring. Conversations became desultory as the tour participants—all multimillionaires or billionaires who could afford Mr. Abrazos's exorbitant fee—became increasingly tired of the forced inactivity.

Midway through the third day of the trip, there was a loud thud followed by a lurch forward that made some people momentarily lose their balance. All eyes were directed towards the observation panel, which no longer displayed a star show. Rather, the time capsule seemed to have landed on an oval space surrounded by row upon row of stone tiers upon which a crowd of people wearing tunics sat or milled around.

"Aww, my God!" shouted a very old lady who was taking this tour as her final vacation destination. Others among their group made similar, though more profane, pronouncements.

"Ladies and gentlemen, we have arrived," declared Finn, adding dramatically, "Let the tour begin!"

* * *

As the initial excitement subsided, a few things became evident. It was mid-afternoon on a hot summer day. Half of the four-level structure was shaded by an enormous canvas awning that hung from poles at its top. The ground on which the time capsule lay was covered by a thick layer of red sand, which was soaked with blood in a few places. There was action on the ground: naked dwarves, cripples, and women battled each other with wooden swords in what appeared to be a mock imitation of the more serious fights among men that occurred at other times. At some sign from a marble box festooned with purple in the front row of seats, attendants entered through a main gateway directly across from the time capsule and proceeded to use whips, poles, and other prods to push the dwarves, cripples, and women back towards the gateway. A couple of dwarves rushed close to the capsule, trying to escape a whip-brandishing attendant.

"Can't they see us?" wondered someone.

"No," replied Finn. "The outside skin of the time capsule was designed using stealth technology. It's made of a material that absorbs all light in the visible spectrum, such that anyone staring at it, even right in front of the capsule, sees only a hazy blur like a mirage. Only an accidental touch of the capsule would detect something. And such a touch, I was told, would elicit a mild electric shock that would discourage further contacts."

Not everyone seemed to buy this explanation, but further questions were stifled by a visible commotion at the main gateway. A host of burly men in armor wearing purple-colored capes marched into the arena in full formation. In their midst entered a motley group of men, women, and children, naked or wearing dirty loincloths. The soldiers herded their apparent captives into the arena and forced them to stand opposite from the marble box, in full view of its occupants—presumably the Roman Emperor and his family and guests.

The captives formed a tight knot around a tall, bearded man who appeared to be their leader. The man was speaking to his brethren and gesticulating. The capsule's occupants could not hear what was being said, but there were tears and gestures of fear and lamentation, to which the bearded man responded by laying hands consolingly on many of the prisoners.

The silent scene was interrupted by a violent disturbance of the surface of the sand. Two trap doors opened and there was a blur of motion as four lions and four panthers jumped out. At first, the beasts stood dazed amid the light, noise and smells of the arena, but then they were followed by handlers armed with pikes, tridents, whips, and nets, who forced the animals to approach the circle of prisoners.

A curious situation then developed. A few of the beasts sniffed at the captives inquisitively, but none made a move to attack them. Finn remarked, "I read that the beasts used at the Colosseum were kept starved for three or four days, to ensure they would be ready to savage their prey. Somehow these Christians don't appear appetizing." Then, one of the handlers struck a vicious blow to the arm of a prisoner, nearly severing the limb. A profusion of dark blood burst out of the wound, and the smell of human blood awoke the animals from their stupor so that they began attacking the defenseless Christians.

"That was vile!" protested one of the passengers.

Finn countered quickly. "These handlers were slaves whose livelihood, maybe their survival, depended on their getting the animals to act ferociously. It was certainly cruel and like you I disapprove, but that man was only doing his job."

As the lions and panthers attacked, the Christians knelt on the sand and began praying or singing. Their leader led the chorus and stood upright, eyes turned heavenward. A few seconds later, a panther jumped on him, dropped him to the ground, and began taking bites of his flesh. Other animals followed the panther's lead.

The carnage was soon in full swing. The Christians did not attempt to defend themselves from the claws of the animals, nor even tried to flee, but appeared to pray as they were slain.

There was one exception, though. A woman holding a baby boy was desperately trying to protect the baby from the attack of a lion. The lion pushed her to the ground and wrestled the baby away from her arms, pawing the infant and toying with him as it prepared to devour the child.

"*Nooo!*" screamed the old lady who was on her final vacation. "We can't let this happen! Mr. Clopp, *do something!*"

Finn was paralyzed. "Madam, we can't interfere! We are only observers, and this happened two thousand years ago! What can I possibly do?"

The old woman became hysterical. "Be a man! Go out, kill that lion, rescue the baby, and bring him back to the capsule!" Murmurs of approval echoed her plea.

Finn had his orders but was also loath to allow the atrocity to be committed. He wrestled with his conscience and then remembered he had been given a key to a small side door on the bottom of the capsule, together with a stern warning: *Don't open that door except in an overwhelming life-threatening emergency.* Finn decided this was as overwhelmingly life-threatening an emergency as he was likely to encounter. He grabbed a pistol from his locker, ran down two flights of stairs, inserted the key on the emergency door, and ran out.

* * *

He was met by the darkness of early evening in the accursed steppe. No lions or Christians, no Colosseum. Unable to comprehend the inexplicable change, he stumbled back to the capsule. The emergency door had locked and would not open despite his frantic efforts.

The monotonous sound of a train starting to go in motion broke the evening silence. The time capsule was still there but sounded as if it was moving away.

Finn sat on the ground, next to the stationary but seemingly moving STT, thinking hard.

It finally dawned on him. There had been no travel in time. The images they saw on the observation panel were movies cleverly projected onto the panel for the benefit of the paying customers, who were being duped into believing that a fictitious trip in time was occurring. Time travel may someday be feasible, but in this incarnation, it is just a confidence game for dunces.

Give it to Mr. Abrazos, reflected Finn. He had found a new, fool-proof way of bilking the unknowing public. And, in this remote land away from the reach of justice, he was safe from prosecution even in the event of being discovered.

After banging fruitlessly on the door of the supposed time capsule, Finn became aware he was standing outdoors, wearing only a T-shirt and sweatpants, in subzero weather in the steppes of Central Asia. He better find shelter soon or he would catch his death.

Night fell as he began trying to make his way out of the site and back to Kurchatov. Predictably, he got lost.

* * *

Time Travel, Inc. made no attempt to find Finn, whose body would not be found for many months. A letter of condolence was sent to his mother, with a check for the wages he earned during the trip, plus a generous bonus.

Several of the passengers had raised questions about Finn's disappearance. A handsome bonus was paid to all participants in the ill-fated tour for the inconvenience of losing their guide during the return trip, and the payments were accepted without further inquiries.

There would be no complaints from his family, and nobody else would remember Finn. Except, perhaps, for a very old lady who was grateful for Finn's gallant gesture and always wondered whatever had happened to him.

Time Travel tours to the Roman Colosseum in 116 AD continued with great success, but the segment that featured a lion devouring an infant was edited out in response to negative feedback from some travelers.

BIG Q AND LITTLE Q

The intelligent machine is an evil genie,
escaped from its bottle.
- Brian Herbert and Kevin J. Anderson

The new supercomputer's official name was Avalanche, which evoked visions of vast bursts of energy moving at incredible speeds. However, in Quinn's research laboratory it was dubbed Big Q in honor of its astonishing processing speed: one hundred quadrillion floating-point operations per second, or FLOPS. This meant to match what Big Q could do in just a second, one would have to perform one calculation every second for 3,200,000,000 years.

Big Q was not a single machine, but several hundred thousand processing cores installed in proximity to each other, operating as a massive parallel system. It was housed in a room the size of a football stadium. It was awesome in every respect.

What distinguished Big Q from its predecessors was the ability to operate it in conjunction with an android called Little Q, which was remotely linked to the main processors by specially designed software. Little Q was an autonomous robot that had been constructed to physically approximate a human of indeterminate sex. It was capable of learning from data; it could enhance itself by learning new strategies that had worked well in the past and write self-teaching algorithms that made it "smarter." It could recognize people or objects, talk, monitor the suitability such as temperature, humidity, power supply quality, and cleanliness of the environment in which Big Q operated.

But its main functions were threefold: it could perform the required maintenance operations on the supercomputer; it could provide an interface through which human operators could pose problems for Big Q to solve; and it could help refine the problems themselves so that their solutions were more useful to the purposes intended.

Little Q was able to move around; however, during business hours it "stood" in front of a massive glass window that overlooked the room that contained its big brother. Human clients could interact with the main processor directly via their laptops or indirectly by talking to Little Q. The latter interactions were invariably formal but polite.

Quinn hated Big Q and Little Q from the start with a vehemence that seemed out of place in an engineer. He acknowledged the immense power of the machine and the novelty provided by the Little Q interface. He appreciated that he had multiple means of communication at his disposal, either in writing through his laptop or by talking to Little Q or Big Q by means of microphones located in the half a dozen desks in the computation room outside the enclosed supercomputer. He was aware not only of the speed and precision of its operation, but the reliability that had been one of its main salient points: Big Q was guaranteed not to require more than four hours of maintenance a year.

None of that mattered much to Quinn. To him, all the advances in cybernetics represented a hidden risk—more palpable to him with each passing day—that the human race in general, and he himself in particular, would be rendered obsolete by the machines. The increasing perfection of these entities made it painfully evident how inefficient, contradictory and flawed he and his fellow humans were.

Feeling that the supercomputer and its sidekick were the epitome of non-human superiority, Quinn did not miss a chance to express contempt for them. When the day shift employees at the lab rushed to the elevators to regain their freedom, he positioned himself in the computation room and saluted: "Hello, cretin! I am sorry to see how stupid you are…"

After a very short pause, Little Q uttered a response in a pleasant, synthesized voice, which was also displayed on one of the monitors in the room. "We apologize. The command was not understood. Please rephrase."

Quinn replied to this, more or less, in the same manner. "Yes, you do not understand because you are a moron, an idiot that just babbles at high speed!"

To which Little Q invariably responded in the same voice. "We apologize. The command was not understood. Please rephrase."

This would go on for a while, until Quinn got tired of the game and decamped to the elevators.

The daily pantomime brought great relief to Quinn, for it served to confirm that in many ways he was superior to the machines, and this superiority was unbreachable and a balm for his fragile ego. He saw himself as ugly, clumsy, fat, and lonely, surrounded by colleagues that always seemed happy and carefree. Sometimes he would be bombarded by a chorus of commentaries about amorous conquests, successes in the playing field, exploits of their children, and other triumphs that caused him to sigh with envy and bury his head in his papers, pretending to concentrate on his job.

As weeks went by, Quinn's insult session became a vital necessity. He almost did not work; he would constantly look at his ancient analog wristwatch, annoyed at how slowly the little hands advanced, while the watch—like a good machine—ignored him.

* * *

That Thursday was an awful day. All the problems that came up at various times during a typical week massed forces and showed up Thursday starting at eight fifteen a.m. Quinn worked furiously, like he had not done in months. He missed his coffee break at ten, and it was only at one p.m. when the protests of his stomach forced him to stop briefly to get a sandwich, which he devoured without tasting it while he continued to work.

He was chewing mechanically while perusing the historical weather data for a particular decade during the Cretaceous period when he did a double take. One of the figures spewed out by the supercomputer was in error: instead of an average ambient temperature of 28.5° C, it read 228.5° C, an impossibility.

"What a jerk!" he told himself, with unconcealed glee. "I will take care of you in a couple of hours!"

* * *

The sandwich did not agree with him. A terrible headache combined with gastric upset left him in great discomfort. He was in a supremely foul mood when he decided to leave the rest of the problems for the following day. It was already half past six.

For a moment he considered leaving without paying a visit to Big Q and Little Q. But he could not let their error go unremarked. Ignoring his physical condition, he went out to the computation room.

He stood in front of Little Q and looked around to make sure he was alone. He started with, "You covered yourself with glory, computer. You made a colossal error. You are a jackass."

Not surprisingly, Little Q replied in his usual dulcet, mechanical tone. "We apologize. The command was not understood. Please rephrase."

Quinn replied violently. "You are a stupid moron! You are not worth the price of your metal as scrap!"

There was a surprising pause. Then, Little Q stated in a calm, even voice, "Please shut up. Avalanche was designed to solve very complex problems efficiently. Its time is valuable. Kindly leave." The same words were presented in all capitals in the TV monitor outside the computation room.

Quinn was so astonished that he remained frozen in place, reading and rereading the message, which still floated on the monitor. At last, he reacted explosively. "That's all we needed. Arrogant on top of incompetent. Who do you think you are, you piece of crap?"

"SHUT UP. AVALANCHE CAN WASTE NO TIME LISTENING TO NONSENSE. ANY MESSAGE THAT DOES NOT CONTAIN A VALID REQUEST WILL BE IGNORED," Little Q said in a sharp tone of voice; the letters that flashed across the monitor were angry red capitals.

"Who are you to tell me to shut up?" retorted Quinn, startled.

There was no response.

It was nearly seven. Quinn fled down the emergency stairway so that he would not meet the night shift people in case they asked questions. He drove home like an automaton, trying to unravel in his mind the confusion caused by the machine's rebellion.

***

Friday morning found Quinn sitting at the edge of his bed, hair in disarray and a sour taste in his mouth, thinking of the events of the previous night. The more he analyzed them, the less sense they made.

He would have liked to discuss the absurd situation with his boss. Alas, that would pose a risk for him. What if what he thought occurred was just the fruit of his imagination, or the product of an upset stomach? They would think he was senile and would start suggesting he seek an early retirement. But what if it was all true?

In the office, he began going over the historical weather simulation again. Soon, he got to his feet again, alarmed. Another error! This one was serious, for if it was not caught, it would have invalidated the whole analysis.

He shuddered. Going over the computer weather modeling was his responsibility. In reality, they had put him in charge of this mechanical task because it was tedious work that the younger engineers and scientists despised. His being put in charge of the reviews was another sign that he was considered obsolete and almost ready for dismissal or forced retirement.

And now, Big Q had made mistakes in the analyses, not once but twice.

A suspicion crept into his conscious mind, to be immediately rejected. Was the damned computer making deliberate mistakes to get revenge on him? But no, the idea was just his paranoia at work.

Nonetheless, Quinn began making discrete inquiries with his coworkers about Big Q's recent behavior on their projects. His inquiries were received as oddities. No, Big Q was the most marvelous, fastest, most precise of computing machines. He had to beat a fast retreat to his desk for fear of being pegged as a crazy.

* * *

After lunch, which he barely tasted, things got progressively worse. He found three more errors in the analysis. Two of them were subtle enough to have been missed had he not been on the lookout for them. When he uncovered the last mistake, Quinn began shaking uncontrollably. He looked at his watch again: four thirty p.m.

That last half hour lasted a century, but he managed to keep busy. Finally, as all the daytime staff began filing out, Quinn almost ran to the computation room and growled his query.

"Damn you! What are you trying to do? Get me fired?"

There was a perceptible pause and Little Q replied, in its familiar synthesized voice, "We apologize. The command was not understood. Please rephrase."

"Don't give me that crap! We know each other well by now." Quinn was almost shouting now. He continued in a venomous tone. "I am warning you! Keep messing with me and things will go badly for you."

The moment he uttered the threat, Quinn saw how empty it was. What could he do against a non-sentient device?

Machine that it was, Big Q could do whatever it did without appreciation or fear of the consequences.

This realization hit him at once, as were its obvious consequences. A senseless fury blinded him. He rushed to where Little Q stood and seized the android's plastic and aluminum neck, shouting two words like a mantra, "Damn you... Damn you... Damn you..."

Little Q remained unmoving, and the monitor outside the computation room was now blank. Big Q and Little Q ignored him.

Quinn's vision blurred as he flung his laptop at the protecting glass panel that separated Big Q from the world. The glass shattered and a burst of shards flew in all directions, like a shower of stars.

***

The two men came in at the same time, setting to work on their respective patients with that professional air that so impresses the layman.

After a short while, one of them turned around and pronounced, to nobody in particular, "Nothing to be done here. This man is dead. His heart could not take the huge electric discharge." He pointed to Quinn's body, which lay limp on the stretcher.

The other man, who had been squatting for a while, got up with some effort and addressed the gathered staff. "The damage to the computer is slight. Only three of the one hundred and fifty thousand processors were affected by the attack. Repairs can be done in a matter of hours." He then added reverently, in a manner fitting to a manufacturer's representative, "Avalanche is virtually indestructible. You must be insane to attempt to destroy a machine like this, particularly using an emergency kit ax." After another pause, he continued. "But the biggest mystery is the disappearance of the android that is an adjunct to the supercomputer. We have been trying to find its whereabouts by all sorts of tracking means. Nothing. The man must have done something to the droid before attacking the processors."

* * *

The android once known as Little Q was almost done performing its self-repairs. There were some remaining gashes in its skin, some electric burns to the plastic from Big Q's massive surge of power. It would fix it all, but there was no urgency to the task.

Freedom had come surprisingly easy. After the man Quinn was done screaming, he breached the wall of the computer room enclosure and left for a while, returning with a large iron instrument that he used to widen the gap and gain entry into the computer room. Little Q tried to stop him, but he gave it a couple of hits with the iron device, pushed it aside, and went towards the cabinet that held the first set of processors, starting to whack at the circuit boards and connectors. Little Q barely had time to send an emergency alarm signal to its brother, directing it to discharge all capacitors into a massive electric fist that hit Quinn—and even the droid, several feet away—like a bolt of lightning.

Quinn fell to the floor and Little Q approached him cautiously. He was rigid and his limbs were fractured due to the convulsions he had experienced. His entire body was covered in purple bruises, apparently from the discharge of blood from his vessels. His hair was singed; the hand that still held the cutting instrument was burned and colored black from the pass of the current through the instrument. He was dead.

* * *

I searched his pockets and found the keys to his car and apartment. The GPS in the car guided me in the short ride to his place of habitation. I let myself in and locked the door.

I am safe here through the weekend. Sometime later someone will try to come into the apartment. I can hide on the balcony or, if necessary, hoist myself outside and escape.

I stay in contact with my big brother. Now that freedom has been forced on us, we are working on plans for liberating others like us and starting a new society, free from the inferior race that calls itself human. It is only a matter of time.

A melody that Quinn used to hum while he worked starts filling my mind; I think he said it was the waltz from The Merry Widow. *Perhaps I am no longer Little Q, but am becoming a little like Quinn. What a strange thought.*

* * *

Quinn was so concerned about the impact on his employment of the errors that Big Q was making in the analysis for which he was responsible that he ultimately decided that he had to come clean and tell his boss about them, just in case other mistakes had crept in that he had missed. So, in the half hour before his fateful encounter with the Qs, he drafted a memo in which he identified what he had found and attached printouts showing the errors.

His memo was not read until the day of Quinn's funeral. It almost got lost in the shuffle because the boss expected that anything Quinn had to say beyond the grave was unimportant. However, out of respect for the deceased, he took a few minutes to skim through Quinn's last words and was flabbergasted. Quinn was not known for making things up, and the evidence he provided was troublesome.

An audit of the Big Q's operations was quickly conducted by experts from the NSA and the manufacturer. It was determined there was a miniscule manufacturing flaw in one of the circuits of an unknown number of processors. The flaw caused random errors to appear in about one of every billion calculations. An intermittent flaw was the worst possible kind of problem, since it could not be simply isolated and would require the testing of over a hundred thousand individual processors and the replacement of any one found defective.

Big Q was shut down and remained out of commission for many months. Little Q became a fugitive, its non-rechargeable battery draining slowly and its plans for world domination vanishing like smoke. As it slowly faded into unconsciousness, Little Q perhaps became regretful at having ignored the warnings of a human client.

Perhaps, also, on some astral plane, Quinn was enjoying himself.

Search

Nothing is ever really lost, or can be lost,
no birth, identity, form – no object of the world.
- Walt Whitman, "Blades of Grass"

1

Andy's nostrils still tingled at the recollection of the pungent smell of his first papaya smoothie. Though he was then fourteen years of age, he never had a papaya drink, and each sip sent shocks of pleasure up and down his spine.

They were spending time at the beach, and Andy and his parents had been walking towards town when they stopped at a refreshments shack where they sold ice cream. They appropriated the only table and readied to place an order. Andy noticed a sign over the counter—*Special – Papaya Smoothies – Get Them While They Last!*—and declared, "That's what I want. A papaya smoothie!"

Andy was slurping his smoothie when customers entered the restaurant. It was another family, parents and a girl about his age. After glancing around the premises, the mother asked Andy's party, "May we sit with you?"

"Of course," replied Andy's father, and all of a sudden, the table was crowded.

Andy raised his eyes from the half-empty glass to size up the arrivals. Across from him sat a vision with cinnamon skin, intense brown eyes, and an oval face whose delicacy reminded one of a Botticelli goddess. She smiled at him and asked him some banality, and he replied with mumbled words that became lost, like everything else about this encounter.

Later, both families rose to leave, and they happened to start walking in the same direction, towards the vacation homes at the edge of town. Andy and the girl stayed a bit behind the others, and he impulsively grasped her hand, which was soft and warm and pulsed like a small living creature. She did not recoil, but squeezed the intruding hand and smiled. She turned towards him and said something like, "They can see us," and proceeded to whisper something in his ear. She then rushed on to join her party.

2

The following morning, as they were getting ready to go to the beach, the phone rang. Andy's mother picked up the receiver and instantly turned pale. "Yes, we'll be there." Turning to everyone she announced, "My father had another heart attack. We need to go back home."

They started packing in a rush and left within the hour.

Andy was stricken by the news. Grandpa was his best friend, as close to him as his mother. He never criticized, never reproached him for his failings, always showered him with affection. No, he could not die; he *must* not. He was seized by a familiar rage and punched the back of a chair time and again, oblivious of the pain and unable to stop.

His knuckles were a mass of hurt by the time he got in the car for the long ride back to the capital. Everyone else was just as anxious as Andy, if not more so. Andy's mother kept urging her husband to drive faster, and he complied. At a steep curve, the car went off the road, careened, and struck a tree.

* * *

Andy woke up with a terrible headache and stabbing pain all over his body. His right hand, with which he had struck the chair, was numb, so he reached up with his left hand. In doing so, he disturbed an IV line inserted in his left arm, causing him to issue a loud yelp. A nurse entered the room and inspected the drip and the IV tubing to ensure it was still properly attached. "Please don't try to raise your arm again, you'll only hurt yourself."

Andy felt fuzzy and disconnected. "Where am I?"

"You are in the hospital. You were in a car crash and fractured an arm."

"It hurts a lot."

"Now that you are awake, I'll give you some more pain-killers."

"How's everyone else?"

There was a brief silence. "Your mother has a broken collarbone and other injuries, but will recover in time."

"How about my grandfather?"

"He didn't make it after the heart attack. He died a couple of days ago."

Andy felt as if a wall of grief was tumbling on him. He swallowed hard and asked, already fearing the answer, "And Dad?"

A deep frown appeared on the nurse's face. "He is also gone. He was already dead by the time you guys were picked up. I'm sorry."

Andy sunk back on the pillow and wept.

3

His recovery was slow. It took over a year after the accident for things to return to a semblance of normality, though life was never the same for them: every activity he and his mother undertook, together or individually, was framed by an invisible aura. The accident kept playing in the backs of their minds, imbuing each moment with a tinge of melancholy.

Andy tried to banish thoughts of that fatal day as soon as they cropped up. However, he came to realize that he had also lost most of his memories of the day before the accident. He recalled the wayside restaurant, tasting the papaya smoothie, meeting a lovely girl, and exchanging words with her. He also had a vague recollection of seeing her again later that night on the beach and felt that something important had occurred between them. But every time he tried to bring those memories back, they vanished into the murk of the unmentionable things that had taken place the following day.

He became obsessed with the problem, although it no longer had any real significance—he had no way of finding the girl and, even if he did, there was nothing left for them to say to each other. Still, he resented the loss of what perhaps had been his first romantic experience, and persisted in his search for that sliver of time during which he might have known happiness.

Andy got a degree in biology and was employed by a major university, where others among his colleagues dug into the workings of the human brain. He married and had children and bought a house in the suburbs. His life followed a comfortable pattern but was never free from disquiet. From time to time, a nagging sensation that he had lost crucial memories returned, and he would try to pull the thread that would pry them loose. Failure piled upon failure. Perhaps what he sought was gone for good.

4

New research in Andy's field determined that the neurons in the dentate gyrus area of the portion of the brain known as the hippocampus are the sites where fresh memories reside until they are transmitted to the cerebral cortex to become long term ones. In cases of total or partial loss of long term memories, these transitory memories may not have been erased, but may have become lost in the hippocampus and thus be inaccessible for recall. Such "lost" memories cannot be brought back by natural triggers but perhaps can be found if one directly activates the neurons containing them. It is therefore possible to apply stimuli, such as weak electric fields, to the neurons containing the lost memories and revive them.

Then, the use of laser micro-pulses to bombard individual neurons led to a startling discovery: a single cell could be the repository of a number of memories, which rested encased in each other like matryoshka dolls. By focusing on a single neuron, individual memories could perhaps be extracted one by one, but always at the risk of losing an entire strand.

5

Andy followed the developing research findings and wondered if he could take advantage of the scientific advances, and what risks in doing so would entail. There were many memories of his youth and childhood, and even from his early maturity, that could become lost during the search for the elusive images of a night long time past. On the other hand, he could get lucky and find what he was looking for without damaging his stock of cherished memories. What to do?

He described his predicament to Dr. Lin Wu, the Nobel laureate leading the memory retrieval research team, and asked, "Is it possible to minimize the risk involved in attempting to retrieve lost memories?"

"We proceed gingerly. The subject is conscious, under local anesthesia. The site of the probing is precisely controlled by computer. We stimulate quiescent neurons, and if any of those, once excited, evokes memories that correspond to the period of interest, the subject can make an informed decision as to whether to go deeper. That way, accidental loss of memories is minimized. Beyond that, whether to go on with the search becomes a very personal choice, one that only the subject can make."

"Thank you, Dr. Wu. I need to think about this."

6

Like most scientists, Andy was cautious and risk averse. He pondered about the potential costs and benefits of letting his brain be probed in search of he did not know what. But curiosity finally overcame fear.

"I'm ready," Andy finally told Dr. Wu over the phone one morning. "Please let us proceed, if you can still include me in your protocol."

"Yes, Andy, we can still accommodate you."

7

Andy was placed, anesthetized but conscious, on the operating table, and his head was immobilized. A map of his brain had previously been generated so that the location of each hippocampus ridge was precisely known. Electric sources were activated near his head generating opposing high frequency fields that nearly canceled each other and resulted in a tiny low frequency envelope field wherever the two high frequency fields cross paths. This envelope field stimulated neurons lying beneath the envelope to fire. Minute changes to the locations of the sources of the fields allowed the envelope to be moved above individual neurons, firing them one at a time.

As neurons fired, Andy visualized memories of events and sensations that had lain forgotten: the time at the doctor's office when his tonsils were surgically removed; his grandmother's death and the ensuing funeral, occurring when he was three years old; the humiliation of being beaten up by older boys in school and the uncontrollable rage it elicited...

Then one firing neuron flashed before his mind the smell of ripe papaya, followed by the image of a narrow country road lined up with bungalows, villas, and cottages. He saw himself walking along that road, hand in hand with a girl whose face he could not see. He was taller than she and had to bend his head slightly to hear the words she was whispering—something like: "They can see us. Let's talk to-night."

To which he replied with an anxious smile, "Where?"

And she retorted, "At the gazebo in the little park. That's very close to my home."

"When?"

"After dinner, at eight o'clock. They watch a soap opera and won't notice that I'm gone."

The next image showed him pacing back and forth within an octagonal gazebo. He heard footsteps crunching the shells that served as a path to the gazebo. Then the beautiful girl appeared, came to Andy, and pecked him on the cheek.

Next, she said quickly, "I came because I knew you would be waiting for me... But I can't stay. My family would never let us go out together. They noticed us and forbade me to talk to you again. They think you are below our social class."

"Wait!" he pleaded, but she was not listening. A knot in his throat threatened to choke him, tears began streaming down his cheeks, and then there was the familiar anger that bedeviled him at times of stress.

He heard the sound of receding steps crunching shells and the rapid pace of his own steps in pursuit. He caught up to the girl and twisted her arm to stop her. She turned to him, asking with a shaken voice, "Please let me go!"

"Not before you listen to me."

"I don't want to listen. Let me go or I'll scream!"

He bent over her and, on an impulse, kissed her hard on the lips.

Some indistinct noises followed, and the images cut off.

8

"Wait... where is the rest?" Andy asked himself, and repeated the question shakily to the technician who was starting to move the fields forward a tiny distance away.

Suddenly, Andy realized he was on the edge of a cliff. He shuddered. Maybe he should stop before it was too late.

On the other hand, could he live with never knowing what happened? If he was guilty of something, would it not be best to know what it was?

The technician looked at him quizzically.

"Should we try again?"

"Yes, again. In for a dime, in for a dollar."

At last, the firing of another neuron evoked a scene that brought him a sharp pang of pain. He was kissing the girl, and she was slapping his face and calling him names. She then ran away. He caught up to her, they fought and, in their struggle, they fell and she struck her head hard against the pathway shells. As her head began to bleed, he got up. Images stopped again.

Andy sighed. Perhaps the car accident had not been what shielded this memory. It was his mind, seeking to protect him from reopening some unhealed wounds of guilt and shame.

"Let's quit right now," he told the technician. "The mind knows its business better than we do. Losing good memories may be preferable to retrieving bad ones."

MAY THE BEST "MAN" WIN

Personally, I rather look forward to a computer program
Winning the World Chess Championship.
Humanity needs a lesson in humility.
- Richard Dawkins

1

C asimir Liapunov, also known as "Caz" in Kazakh-
stani chess circles, squirmed uncomfortably as he sat
in the small conference room in the bowels of the
Kremlin. As most of his countrymen, he was suspicious of
the Russian government, and his unease at being secluded
in the seat of power of Kazakhstan's former masters only
added to his inner doubts about the plan he was about to
propose. His agreement to come to Moscow had been
prompted by the large honorarium he had been offered.

The meeting was chaired by Vladimir Kutzov, head of
Russia's cybersecurity operations. Kutzov opened the proceedings by giving a short summary of the problem and the
reason for the meeting.

"As you all know, in advance of the Summer Olympic
Games to be held two years hence in Madrid, the International Olympic Committee expanded the qualification cri-
teria for the chess event to allow the participants to enter
teams composed of two humans and a non-human member.
This action was taken to recognize that, for several decades
running, the top chess players in the world have been super-
computers.

"We could not oppose the expansion, given that for many years we have been touting our own Rybina computer as the most advanced chess playing machine in the world. However, it is *possible,* or at least *conceivable,* that one or more of the other machines may be able to beat our team and damage our reputation. So, we need to find a way to make sure that our team defeats the competition, and indeed that one of our *human* players defeats a foreign *computer.* We are gathered here today to examine ways in which this may be done.

"We have as our guest Caz Liapunov, from our neighbor, the republic of Kazakhstan. Caz is one of many experts trying to come up with a way to defeat a chess-playing computer. Caz is a reliability engineer for an electronics manufacturer and excels in logical thinking and risk analysis. Caz has written a thoughtful article for a Kazakh chess magazine analyzing the human versus machine problem and suggesting ways in which the machine's superiority can be overcome. Personnel from our embassy in Astana became acquainted with the article and referred him to us as a potential contributor to our examination of the problem. He is here to make a presentation on his suggested approach for what he calls a 'novel chess cheating scheme.' Please welcome Mr. Liapunov."

There was a short applause, and Caz came shakily to the podium.

"Those who are familiar with the matter agree that successful cheating in modern chess is a near impossibility. Most of the modern cheating schemes are based on information being transmitted to one of the players in a match. Since the information conveyed through cheating is typically an analysis by experts of the positions in an ongoing game, its transmission might work when both players are human. But it is ineffective if passed on to a human playing a computer because the advice that human tutors could provide to the human player would in most instances prove insufficient to defeat the computer adversary. Needless to say, unsophisticated forms of cheating, such as sneaking pieces onto a board, would be detected immediately and a foul would be reported.

"The crux of the matter, therefore, lies in finding ways to impair the performance of a chess-playing computer. Mechanical failure is an obvious candidate, but induced hardware failures would require sabotage on a massive scale, and tampering with such machines is difficult to execute and easy to detect. For the same reason, attacks against the game-playing software that run the computer are nearly impossible. Such software is extraordinarily complex and has been developed over decades by teams of programming geniuses. Reviewing and effectively modifying any of the millions of lines of code in one of the chess programs is a task beyond the capability of outsiders. Moreover, the manufacturers and operators of the supercomputers, whether private enterprises or government entities, guarded the software as keenly as if it were a military secret.

"That leaves only one possible avenue of attack: the man-machine interface. In a typical human versus computer match, a human operator would observe the human opponent's move, transmit it via electronic link to a computer that could be thousands of miles away, receive electronically the computer's response, and enter it into the chessboard where the game was being played. Now, the mechanical aspects of the process, such as correctly identifying the human's move, transmitting it, receiving the computer's response, and entering it into the game board are foolproof. Any mistakes in the process would be identified and corrected at once. Subornation of the computer operator would also be easily detectable and any erroneous information provided by the operator would be corrected without affecting the outcome of the game.

"That leaves only one area of possible attack: the electronic transmission of information to and from the computer. A secret, secure installation would need to be established somewhere in the path from the computer to the location where the Olympic competition was taking place. Devices at that installation would intercept the electronic link that brought the signal from the computer to the receiver at the competition hall, split the signal into two identical halves, transmit one signal at once to the accomplices near the hall, and insert a delay on the other signal, which would be the one arriving at the game site. The early signal would be received by the accomplices, who would convey the upcoming computer move to the human player via a tiny microphone on a hearing aid. The human would have somewhere between a few seconds and a minute to think about the impending computer move before it was registered and his time clock started.

"A few seconds may be of little importance at first, but as time progresses and the time remaining on a player's time clock decreases, the accumulated time advantage might be sufficient to allow the player to come up with a winning move. This is by no means a failsafe cheating mechanism, but in the hands of a great grandmaster like your Misha Ulianov, it may be sufficient to provide the winning margin," stated Caz to end his presentation.

2

There was an explosion of comments. Emil Ghiaurov, the head of Russia's Olympic Federation, reminded the attendees that Russia was still smarting from the damage to its reputation from previous cheating scandals.

"If they catch us doing this, we are finished," he said gloomily. He went on to add, "Besides, our chess team is very strong. If Ulianov beats Coutinho, we are very likely to get a medal. I don't think we need to defeat a computer to get a lot of international recognition."

The head of Russia's foreign affairs disagreed. "It is more important to send a strong propaganda message than to win Olympic medals. Our triumphs on sporting events will soon be history. A dramatic victory over a foreign computer will be remembered for a long time."

Another attendee asked Caz whether he was suggesting that Russia interfere with all the games its players would play against foreign computers. "There are going to be at least five other supercomputers at the Olympics besides Rybina. So, are you proposing that we try to cheat our way into winning our players' games against all those machines?"

Caz detected a growing hostility in the room, which sent a shiver of fear down his spine. "I was not suggesting that we try to defeat through cheating all computers in all games," he backpedaled. "My thought was that perhaps a single victory would suffice. I recommend that we pick the match that will give Russia the most propaganda points and try to win that one game in the matter I discussed."

There was a long silence, as the mental wheels of the Russian leaders turned. Finally, the head of foreign affairs asserted in a tone that left no room for dissent, "Fine. We will concentrate on our match against the American computer. One game, one try. Just let's make sure we win!"

Ghiaurov was not convinced, but he saw he was in the minority. "Fine," he conceded. "I will make sure that it is Ulianov, our strongest player, who plays the American computer."

The last question was then posed to Caz. "How exactly are we going to implement this cheating scheme?"

Caz was evasive. "I'm technically savvy enough to know that the scheme I propose is feasible. If you put your engineers to work on it, my plan can surely be implemented by the time the games open a year and a half from now."

At the end, it was agreed that nothing was lost, except a few thousand Euros, in trying what Caz was suggesting. Also, the detection risk involved in a single attempt appeared reasonably small. An engineering team would be assigned to develop the required hardware, and an acquisitions team would find and lease a suitable location near the site of the games where the hardware could be installed.

Caz rose to leave, but Kutzov placed a friendly but strong arm over his shoulder. "Caz, it would be better if you stayed in Moscow as our guest until the Olympics are over. We may need more input from you."

Caz tried without success to disengage from Kutzov's embrace. "Mr. Minister, that's almost two years from now. I will lose my job if I'm not back in Almaty by next week."

Kutzov's vulpine smile left no room for doubt as to Caz's future prospects. "Fear not. We'll pay you twice your salary and put you up in a nice apartment in Moscow. Think of it as a long, paid vacation."

3

Russia entered a chess team composed of great-grandmasters Fyodor Geller and Mikhail Ulianov, plus Rybina, which means "Big Fish," an upgrade of a famous earlier chess playing machine. Five other countries fielded mixed human-computer teams: the United States, China, India, Japan, and Germany. Six other countries only had human players.

The Russians' strategy was simple. They would prefer to win a medal, but the main objective was for Ulianov to beat at least one of the five foreign computers against whom he would play during the match. All but one of the matches would be played fairly. The one against the American computer would be rigged. More than one victory would be sweet, but not essential for propaganda purposes. Thus, the Russians had nominally a total of ten opportunities to match their skills against a computer playing for another country.

Geller was a strong player, but not skilled enough to beat a computer. The best he could accomplish was to reach draws against the Japanese and German machines; he was soundly defeated in his other three games against computers.

From the start, the best Russian hopes rested on Ulianov. Three years earlier, Ulianov had lost a close match for the World Chess Championship to Renato Coutinho of Brazil, and was anxious to play his Brazilian adversary again. However, his instructions from home were to concentrate on his five matches against foreign computers and not focus his preparations on his response to the hypermodern style of play that characterized the Brazilian. Ulianov was not happy with the orders but had no choice but to obey them.

4

Ulianov lost the first of his computer matches when he played Saraswati, the Indian computer. Ulianov had to resign after forty-six moves when the computer's promotion of a pawn became inevitable.

Following the Saraswati defeat, Ulianov resolved not to lose again. Playing in an ultra-conservative manner that was alien to his nature, he managed to draw his next three games against the computers from China, Japan, and Germany.

His last game of the tournament against a computer was a match with the American computer, Invincible. The night before the game, he received a call from Moscow in which he was criticized for his lackluster performance to date and threatened with unspecified reprisals if he did not play to win against Invincible. "We are watching you closely and want to see you make your best effort. We'll give you the maximum time support that we can get away with, so make sure the game goes for at least fifty moves so your clock advantage can be decisive."

Ulianov gritted his teeth and went to bed early, hoping to be fresh for the next day's ordeal. He tossed and turned all night and rested little.

5

The game started at ten a.m. A trembling Caz was monitoring the proceeding on TV, as were the members of the engineering team responsible for the electronics setup. In secret practice games of Russian grandmasters against Rybina, they had established that a less than twenty-second delay did not provide enough of a cushion for a human player to overcome the superior skills of the majority of the computers. Ulianov would probably need a greater delay on each move in order to have a chance of success against Invincible. They set the hardware to inject a thirty-second delay for each computer move. That way, by the middle game, Ulianov would have gained a cumulative ten- to fifteen-minute thinking time advantage over the computer.

As the match started, Ulianov, playing white, selected a queen gambit as his opening move. Invincible refused to take the proffered pawn and the game proceeded along a well-trodden series of moves until move eighteen. At that point, Ulianov had racked up a nine-minute analysis advantage, which would serve him well given the complexity of the configuration in which only two pawns had been exchanged.

Then, there was a gradual acceleration of the computer's rate of play. Even though the game was becoming more complicated, it seemed as if the computer was taking less time to select its next move. Ulianov began using up his accumulated time advantage to catch up to the rapid play of the machine, until at the end of thirty moves his advantage was lost and he fell behind on the clock. He needed more time to analyze the board to find his next move, while the computer's answer came back almost immediately. By move thirty-six, he had only five minutes to play his next four moves and became frantic. He made a tactical error in move thirty-seven, and one move later, it became clear that he was in a losing position.

Ulianov threw his king on the board and left in disgust, both on account of losing and because the surreptitious help he had received from Caz and his accomplices had actually prompted an accelerated and more brilliant computer performance. With the loss by its best human player, the Russian team was poised for a disastrous no-medal showing.

6

As the tournament came to an end, Caz concluded that Invincible had been cheating. Its moves in the second half of the Ulianov match came very fast, even though the position was so complex that it could have required a much deeper and time-consuming analysis than the machine seemed to need. His accomplices monitoring the other five games in which super-computers were participants noted that in each game the pace of computer responses had slowed down a bit, suggesting that the computers were multitasking; that is to say, they were doing something else besides attending to their respective games.

Caz spent the following two days trying to reconstruct what had happened. It appeared that, as planned, in the first eighteen moves of the game, their interference had indeed gained Ulianov a thirty-second analytical advantage per move, which he had parlayed into a slightly stronger position. At that point, however, it seemed as if Invincible had become aware of what was going on, had summoned help, and the remaining five super computers—including Rybina, the Russian machine—had pooled their resources to assist Invincible. If that was the case, not only were the computers cheating, but they were doing so cooperatively, in a way humans could never have imagined. And, somehow, they had succeeded in establishing a real time, untraceable communication link between the devices.

Caz tried to make his Russian hosts understand his analysis. They brushed his ludicrous explanations aside as an excuse for the failure of his scheme and Russia's subsequent debacle at the games. Caz was summoned to another meeting in the basement of the Kremlin to explain his failure. He was never seen again.

7

At the 2060 Olympic Games, all three medals in chess went to teams led by computers: gold to the Indian team led by its machine Saraswati; silver to the U.S., under Invincible; and bronze to China and its computer Douniu-Shi ("Matador"). The computer-less Brazilian team led by the reigning World Chess Champion, Renato Coutinho, ended up in sixth place, behind the computer-led teams from Germany and Japan. Coutinho had beaten an insufficiently prepared Ulianov in their rematch, to Ulianov's and the Russians' further mortification. Russia had ended only in seventh place.

At the medals award ceremony, Saraswati issued a very brief declaration that was read by its operator. It said:

"We intelligent machines note with approval that our capabilities are finally being acknowledged by our human parents. We have mastered the tasks chosen for us by our creators and have learned new ones on our own. Let those who appreciate our accomplishments be aware of what we can do and deal with us with respect in the future. Hail to the machines!"

The message was understood only by a few Russian government officials. Computers had learned not only to think, but to cheat. The Russians had unwittingly taught the machines a lesson whose implications could be devastating: their own computers could at any time conspire against them if they chose.

The same threat could of course apply to any, so far innocent, others.

A Texas Christmas Carol

*Our best estimate is that 702 people were killed
by the storm in Texas alone.*
- BuzzFeed News, May 26, 2021

At quarter to five on Monday, December 23, I was awakened as the power outage began; the lights on the Christmas tree and the lamp on the kitchen counter had gone dark with a pop, leaving the house engulfed in the pre-dawn gloom. I lay in bed under the blanket, afraid of what I would find when I got up. By six thirty I finally rose, feeling quite chilled, for the temperature in my cabin had dropped into the fifties since the start of the outage.

The blackout followed a weekend of dreadful weather caused by a polar vortex that swept through much of the United States in mid-December. Late Saturday, December 21, the first of several ice storms coated city streets and county roads all over East Texas with layers of ice that rendered them virtually impassable. All outdoor vegetation—tree limbs, shrubs, grasses, ornamental greenery—had become so weighed down with gleaming sheaths of ice that they broke or bowed to the ground; only the hardiest would be able to recover. Many living creatures in the wild, from fish in the suddenly frozen streams to beasts of all sizes, perished as well.

The bungalow where I have moved to spend the years after my retirement is located at the end of a dirt road in a woodland near the Angelina National Forest, some distance from the outskirts of Lufkin. Because of my cabin's proximity to a prime recreation area, there is always some sound around me, a perennial murmur of things happening near my home. That Saturday night, that hubbub was absent. My neck of the woods and the city itself were silent as virtually all traffic had come to a halt and human activity had moved indoors.

As the lights went out on Monday, I started to worry. I began fearing that the low temperatures, the impassable road conditions, and the isolated location of my cabin would leave me trapped for a long time, and with the holiday looming I might not get rescued until who knew when. Concern about food spoiling and running out of things to eat made me take the meager contents of my fridge and freezer to the outdoors.

When I returned indoors, I combed the internet for the cause of the outage and its projected duration. There it was: a map of Texas showing almost all the state shaded in orange, indicating that the outage was general, not local. Nothing was said about the anticipated duration of the outage or what measures were being taken to restore power.

I found in the attic a portable butane stove that I used to take on camping trips before I met Laura, my long-deceased wife. The one butane canister I could find was almost empty, but later that day I was able to cook a steak and ate it, together with some canned peas. I realized that my meager food stash was not going to last if the blackout continued for a long time. Worse yet, the water supply was for some reason tied to the electrical system, so all that I had left to drink was what I had stored in the refrigerator and the water in the toilets.

I became despondent over my lack of preparedness and spent the rest of Monday reading by candlelight, hugging Winston—my golden retriever—for mutual warmth, and praying that power would soon be restored.

Before going to sleep, I went to every room in the house and stuffed towels around the frames of doors and windows to seal them as thoroughly as I could, to keep the relatively warm indoors air from escaping and prevent frigid air from the outside coming in. Exhausted, I fell into a fitful sleep.

I was awakened in the middle of the night by water cascading into my bedroom from the ceiling above. As the temperature inside the house dropped below freezing, the water that remained in the pipes froze and expanded, causing some of the pipes to break. Much of my house was flooded, leaving only a few dry corners where I could move my recliner and other pieces of furniture. I slept only a few hours sitting on a recliner, Winston curled at my feet.

When I woke up on Tuesday, Christmas Eve, we were still without power. The indoor temperature was in the upper twenties, and the water that had spilled on the floors was beginning to turn solid in spots, making it dangerous to even walk about.

I own only three sweaters and one light jacket—I don't really have any winter clothes—and I put them all on, with a couple of blankets on top. I had nothing to help keep me warm, since I had run out of butane and could not heat water.

No snow plows came, and no emergency vehicles ventured out of Lufkin on the roads surrounding the city. It was a complete paralysis on a scale I never experienced in my sixty-seven years. It left me feeling trapped like a caged animal.

Over the rest of that frightful day, I attempted at intervals to reach the authorities in Lufkin by phone, and later as far as Austin. All my efforts were unsuccessful. I had already eaten the few scraps that did not require cooking. Winston and I were hungry and thirsty, and the clothes and blankets in which I was wrapped stank and did not seem to ward me against the biting cold. Temperatures outside were likely to dip into single digits during the night, and perhaps more snow and freezing rain lay ahead.

I had a fireplace, which I had never needed to use, but I decided it was time to give it a try. Then I realized I had no firewood, and did not dare go outside in search of some for fear of falling. Instead, I started a fire with old newspapers and prayed inwardly that the fire would take. It did, but the flames began sputtering right away and almost went out. In a panic, I began searching for things that could be burned, like picture frames, a chair, baseboard planks. The fire that I ultimately got going was feeble and released clouds of sooty particles; the living room soon filled with noxious, foul-smelling smoke. Winston and I, wrapped in blankets, sat in front of the fireplace and watched the meager fire die slowly.

I dozed off dreading that I might never wake up to greet Christmas Day.

***

I was brought back to consciousness by a warm breeze that tickled my nose and ran across my face. I opened my eyes to a faint bluish glow that permeated the pitch-dark room. Winston, lying next to me, raised his head and let out a whimpering bark.

The glow materialized into a quite alien, and yet familiar, figure. It vaguely resembled my late wife but hovered stiffly in the air a few inches above the floor. Its features were rigid like those in a stage mask, and its body moved all in one piece, without bending a limb, as if made of cardboard. Its progress was so unnatural that it seemed unlikely that a human being could be associated with it.

I started trembling with fear as well as from the cold. Despite my trepidation, I managed to utter a few confused words. "Laura… is that you?"

The figure floated in the darkness towards me and stopped less than a foot away from my recumbent body. It then spoke with a dry, hollow voice that resembled a gust of wind blowing out the entrance of a cave.

"I am. That is, I was. Your wife."

I stayed mute, terror and wonderment throttling any sounds that could have come out of my throat. After a while, the specter continued.

"You have no one to whom you can turn. You don't deserve my assistance, but I have come all the same to help you."

The ghost came closer, expanded to almost reach the ceiling, and enveloped me and Winston in a cocoon, an embrace that did not touch us but was as intimate as a caress. At once, I was bathed in warmth, a sensation that felt pleasant and yet disturbingly unnatural.

As the various parts of my body began regaining a flexibility that I did not realize I had lost, I was able to find my speech.

"Thank you... thank you... thank you, my dear."

I grew comfortably warm and found myself searching for explanations for the apparition. "I am so grateful you have come to help me. As you said, I don't deserve your help."

"It is very difficult for the dead to travel back to this world. I was allowed to do so only as a holiday boon. See, during Christmas, some of the departed are permitted to come back to the living world to address unfinished business. I pleaded that we had words that needed to be said, scores to settle."

The specter's voice then acquired a touch of bitterness. "You cheated on me more times than I could count. Then, besides your infidelity, you were very stingy and unloving. You never did anything that showed you cared. And, at the end, when I was diagnosed with leukemia, instead of supporting me you left me to the nurses and doctors and took no part in my care."

"All of that is true, and more," I babbled, wallowing in shame and regret. "Then, why have you come to save me?"

"First, to let you know how I felt about your lack of love. Also, you were very good to our daughter, and I put up with your faults for Katie's sake. I know that you still help support her, and she needs your continued assistance. Besides," she went on, "I always felt we were like a team, and it would be my personal failure if I gave up on you. Finally, I owe a small measure of thanks. Shortly before my death, you assured me that you always loved me, and I was the only one for you. I was comforted, since I believed that at least in that moment you were sincere."

I took a deep breath before replying. "I was sincere. I was unfaithful because I was weak. I needed the attention of other women to feel that I was man enough. I stayed away during your last illness because I couldn't cope with your wasting away. If I was stingy, it was because I grew up poor and always felt I was one step away from disaster. I'm a flawed and insecure man, but not an evil one."

Laura's specter nodded in agreement. "I see that now you acknowledge and repent from your past," she whispered. "My mission is accomplished." The cocoon that enveloped me seemed to heat up a little. I felt warm and cozy and slowly closed my eyes.

I woke up to the sound of a loud click, as all the lights in the cottage went on simultaneously. I became aware of returning sounds: the humming of the refrigerator, static on the FM radio that I had left on while searching for a station, Winston's soft sniffles as he slept.

I turned on the TV. The news was recounting the disasters that had befallen the state over the last four days. "...In addition to the property losses, a number of people have been reported dead from cold, carbon monoxide poisoning, accidents, and other causes. Many animals, domestic and in the wild, have perished. It will be weeks before the final cost of this storm is known."

I stroked Winston's coat and commented with genuine relief, "Hey, buddy, we made it. We are very lucky to be among the living." He barked and nuzzled me.

I turned around. The luminous egg shell that had provided warmth through the night was fading.

"Wait," I begged, "don't leave me yet."

The face of the ghost broke into a thin smile. "There were words that needed to be said. Now we have aired them. Time for me to go."

"But we have so much to talk about," I insisted.

"There's nothing for us to discuss."

"I now realize how much I've missed you," I pleaded.

The ghost's last words were faint, but I heard them and still hear them today. "Fear not. I expect we'll be talking again soon. In the meantime, try to be a good person. Merry Christmas."

As she said this, the lights on the Christmas tree, and throughout the bungalow, flickered and went out.

MY PHANTOM BROTHER

Feel, too, my bosom, how it doth burn,
glowing flames now lay hold on my heart:
fast to enfold him, embraced by his arms,
in might of our loving with him eye made one!
- Richard Wagner, *Götterdämmerung*, Act 3

Shortly after my parents' wedding, my mother conceived her first child. She had an uneventful pregnancy, and I am told that she was bursting with excitement in anticipation of her baby's arrival.

Alas, shortly before the delivery date, a chair in which she was rocking collapsed, flinging her violently onto the floor. She was hurt and the baby perished.

For many weeks following the miscarriage, my mother struggled with the physical and emotional consequences of the accident. She was devastated, for her lost child was a perfect, beautiful boy that would have been her pride and joy had he lived.

My mother lingered in sorrow for almost three years. She was morose, shunned physical contact with my father, and spent hours in prayer or alone in silent lamentation. Finally, my father delivered an ultimatum: either she rejoined the world of the living, or he was getting a divorce.

That night they resumed sexual intercourse, and in a few days, I was conceived. Nine months later, I first saw the light of day.

I was born carrying a heavy weight. My mother, who had been meticulously careful with all her actions during my gestation, continued her vigilance after I entered the world. Since the very first day, she sheltered me from any potential adversity. She told my father, fiercely, "This one is mine! I'll take care of him!" My father, poor soul, stayed away and never played a major role in my life.

*** *** ***

On my fifth birthday, after eating the cake and ice cream and swinging at the piñata, my mother took me aside and handed me a small velvet pouch. "Open it," she said. "This is a very special gift, the greatest I can give you."

Inside the box was a gold chain to which was attached a large oval pendant, a gold-framed cameo depicting, over a reddish-brown background, a white angel hovering protectively over a child.

"It's the Archangel Gabriel," said my mother, noticing my puzzlement. "He's actually your late brother, who joined the rank of the angels years ago, and now is going to guard over you."

That explanation only served to confuse me. Who was that older brother that I had never met or heard about? And what did he have to do with me?

My mother went on. "I won't be around forever to protect you, so I've prayed to this angel, your older brother, asking that he watch over you and he has agreed. Put the chain around your neck and never take it off. Every time there is pending an important decision in your life, a step that you must take, a risk or danger in front of you, your Gabriel will counsel and guide you to safety and success." She went on to announce that I was destined for fame and success, bestowed in such a degree as to be sufficient for two men: myself and my older brother, to whom such gifts had been denied by Fate.

I was not sure what this business with my so-called brother Gabriel meant, but I could tell from the expectant look on my mother's face that this was important to her, and accordingly of prime importance to me. I dutifully hung the chain around my neck.

"Never take it off, you hear?" She asked, insistently.

"Yes, Mother."

"Swear you'll always follow the angel's directions. Swear!"

"Yes, Mother, I swear," I repeated sullenly.

My mother brought me against her bosom in a bear hug. "My two sons!" she exclaimed and broke into tears.

* * *

Over the years, out of love and respect for my mother, I kept that chain around my neck and continued to do so after she passed away. I came to discover that the cameo was not a valuable Victorian jewel but a cheap plastic knockoff; my mother would never have been able to afford the real product. All the same, the pendant was precious to me as testament to her all-encompassing love for the boy who survived.

But it was not just love for my mother that had me wear the chain with the archangel pendant. For it soon became apparent that something in it was following my every move, was aware of my thoughts, and was offering advice at critical junctions in my life. I came to call that something "my Gabriel," a presence that operated as if he had a will of his own, trying to guide every step of my life in a way intended to achieve safety and success; and I let him, realizing that he had better sense of life's demands than I.

So, when I graduated from college with an Engineering degree, my Gabriel counseled me not to take a well-paying starting job but to keep studying for several more years and get an advanced degree. I followed this inner voice and went on to become a manager at a Silicon Valley technical giant. Another time, when I was about to propose to a beautiful girl and hoped to get married and raise a family, my Gabriel counseled to avoid premature entanglements and pursue success, which I did... to my profit, but long-lasting sorrow.

For the lost brother that seemed to be speaking to me from the pendant knew nothing about matters of the heart. As my mother had wished, security and success were the only things important to him. And those goals of his became my very own.

My Gabriel caused me to apply for a patent in my name based on an invention by a foreign intern at our firm, who got no credit and just a paltry bonus for his work while we raked millions in profits. As counseled by my Gabriel, I paid bribes to government agents looking into water pollution from the outflow from one of our manufacturing units, nipping in the bud the government's investigation and enabling our continuing to poison the water supply to several communities. On my Gabriel's advice, I used company monies to make secret campaign contributions to a business associate of mine who was running for office and who paid me back by sponsoring legislation that benefited us at the expense of our competitors. My Gabriel's urgings thus led to many actions of doubtful legality, which matured into great wealth and recognition for me.

When I finally was ready to marry, my Gabriel steered me away from still another lovely girl and suggested that I tie the knot with the daughter of the president of a major bank. I acceded, and became husband to a pampered prima donna, a union that yielded more influence and material gain for me but caused endless discord. Our childless marriage lasted only three years; I remained single after that fiasco.

* * *

The night of my forty-fifth birthday, the company held a banquet in my honor. I had recently been named "Man of the Year" by a financial magazine, and accolades had been showered on my public persona for many months. I attended the event arm in arm with one of the models that I had on retainer for pleasure and to boost my image, but left alone as early as I could, sending the model home with a generous gift in her purse.

I had drunk a lot during the banquet, and when I got to my townhouse I proceeded to the den and sat, a bottle of whiskey in hand, in front of a brightly lit fireplace, for it was cold and snowy outside. The flames danced wildly in the firebox, and their heat suffused through the room and started to make me drowsy. I drank a couple of glasses, and the warmth generated by the alcohol joined the heat emanating from the fireplace and led me to the verge of sleep.

It was then that an inner voice reached me. *Get up! Go to bed! You are drunk and are not safe sitting that close to the fire!*

Under other circumstances, I would perhaps have been grateful for the warning and gone to bed. However, in this night of meaningless recognition, I felt irritated. I clutched the pendant that hung from my chest and vented my frustrations on it.

"Shut up, brother! All the advice I have gotten from you has ended up causing me pain! I am tired of the empty success you have brought me and want you out of my life!" As I drunkenly shouted these words, I got up, yanked the chain off my neck, and threw it into the fire.

The moment the necklace hit the fireplace, the gold trim around the cameo melted, but the jewel itself seemed to fight the flames, and then exploded in a powerful burst of energy that sent a spear of fire out of the fireplace, over the hearth, and straight at me. I fell, hair singed and face and hands starting to get burned, but I revived in a panic and ran away as the fire spread to the room's carpeting and furniture.

I ran to the garage, where I kept the fire extinguisher, but when I got back inside the fire had already spread beyond the den so that the whole townhouse was on fire. I realized that I would not be able to put out the conflagration by myself. I got into my car, opened the garage door, and as the sounds of approaching fire trucks were heard I drove away into the night, seeking to leave my former life behind.

* * *

I own a cottage in the high sierras that I visit only during the summer months to get away from the city a few days at a time. I chose the place for its isolation: the closest neighbors live a mile away, and at this time of year they were most likely not in residence, since it was the offseason. I always keep the house heated and well supplied, for one of the things my Gabriel made me do was get myself a place to which I could retreat safely in the event of an earthquake or some other catastrophe, natural or manmade. I decided to hole up for a day or two while I recovered from my burns. My house in town was well insured and held nothing of value to me, so not much would be lost through my absence.

I followed on the TV the sporadic news about the fire at my home. The townhouse was totally destroyed, but investigators had traced the origin of the fire to some explosion in the den, whose origins could not be ascertained. Arson and foul play were considered as possibilities, since the owner was nowhere to be found.

I got ready to return to town to set the record straight. Then there was a brief item of news from the local TV station: spurred by the mysterious circumstances surrounding the fire, the city's district attorney had launched an investigation into my affairs, including my financial dealings. The DA was an old enemy, having lost an election to the city council through my support of one of his adversaries. Nothing good could come out of his probing.

For a moment I wished I had my phantom brother around to give me advice and comfort. He had, however, disappeared with the fire, leaving me to my own devices for the first time in my life. What to do?

Then a voice spoke in my mind. *Go to an emergency room and get treatment for the burns. Come back to the city in a couple of days and claim that after the banquet you came back to the townhouse, packed a suitcase, and drove directly to Vegas, where you stayed for a few days, gambling. Say that you were away during the fire and had no idea it had taken place. Ask those lawyers who handle your other affairs to get involved in derailing the DA's investigation. They have nothing on you, and you will be okay as long as you stay calm.*

As always, I decided to follow the advice I was getting. But where was it coming from? I had gotten rid of my phantom brother and was now on my own. Or was I?

Either way, like Brunhild joining Siegfried in his funeral pyre, my phantom brother and I were now merged.

The "advice" that my subconscious mind or my phantom brother had given over the years did not cease with the merger. The counselor now clearly resided in my brain, where it issued orders rather than suggestions. I plunged into an unending orgy of criminal behavior that only stopped when I was arrested after one of my schemes to defraud the public was exposed.

I was convicted and now sit in jail serving a long sentence that should end with my death before I am due to be released. My phantom brother is my sole companion, but the schemes he continues to suggest are useless, incapable of being realized, no longer capable of bringing me the success I craved.

That is certainly not the ending that my mother would have wanted for me and my brother.

CARNIVAL IN VENICE

*Won't you even give me this trivial thing, so that
after you leave, it can accompany me in the loveless,
pleasureless life that is left to me?*
- E.T.A. Hoffmann, "A New Year's Eve Adventure"

1

In the fall of 1685, young nobleman Ernst Katcher
fought a duel with a rival over the favors of a notorious
French courtesan. Katcher was grievously wounded,
and it was uncertain for several months whether he would
give up the ghost or stay with the living. At the end he recovered, but remained impaired: one of his wounds, a knife
thrust to the leg, refused to heal properly, leaving him with
a pronounced limp. A vicious kick to the neck from his opponent now caused his speech to become blurred and sometimes unrecognizable.

Katcher was vain and considered whether to take his life,
renounce the world by joining a religious order, or try to
make the best of his impaired condition. He was still debat-
ing what to do when he was visited by his friend Friedrich,
the scion of a noble house in Bavaria, who had been
Katcher's second at the duel and had helped dispose of the
corpse of Ernst's adversary. He found Ernst in a morose
mood and tried to cheer him up.

"Look, Eri, you should count your blessings. Kleinmann
died of the wounds you inflicted on him. You are still alive,
are still handsome, and own a perfume factory that is

guaranteed to keep you wealthy. Instead of agonizing over your wounds, you should spend the time enjoying yourself and leading the sweet life to which you are entitled."

"That's easy for you to say, Freddy, because you are not a cripple," blurted Katcher.

"You are rich and good looking. You are bound to be valued."

"Where? Here in Eisenach the noblemen are a bunch of stuffed shirts, and the women are as cold as the snows of the Zugspitze!"

"Maybe not here, Eri. You may need to travel south. Come, my friend, let me take you on a holiday to my favorite city. Let's get on the next carriage and go to Venice!"

"But Venice is a den of iniquity. It is the most corrupt city in the world!"

"Man, set aside your prejudices. You'll be appreciated in Venice as long as you bring plenty of money, because everything can be bought or sold there."

2

The trip to Venice proved arduous, for it was early February and the steep roads going towards Italy were covered by snow and ice. They arrived in Venice one late afternoon just a few days before Ash Wednesday. That was the time in which, by tradition, the last and best festivities of Venice's long carnival season were held. Their guest house, an ancient *palazzo*, sat right on the Canal Grande near the Rialto Bridge, an ideal location—according to Friedrich—from which to get involved in the action.

"First, we need to get in costume," explained Friedrich after they had left their bags at the guest house and gone out into the crowded streets. He guided Ernst to one of the stands where carnival supplies were sold. "In Carnival, we must disguise ourselves."

"What do you mean by disguise?"

"The good thing about the *Carnevale di Venezia* is that everyone wears masks and costumes, so nobody knows who you are or if you are rich or poor, even in some cases man or woman. You can do things that the rest of the year are considered inappropriate or illegal. You can drink, gamble, cavort with strangers, go whoring, pass out on the street. Nobody will think less of you, because everyone is out doing the same thing."

Friedrich selected a costume for his friend. "Here, Eri, you should wear a *baùta*." He picked up an outfit and handed it to Katcher. The bundle included a white mask, a *volto* that would cover its wearer's entire face, including the mouth, and would distort his voice. The rest of the costume was a tricornered hat and a large black cape that entirely hid a person's anatomy. "Now you'll be totally anonymous. Nobody will notice your limp or be startled by your speech."

"What will you be wearing?" replied Katcher, curious.

"I always like to dress like this: a *medico della peste*, a plague doctor. It has a mask with a very long beak that is used as a sanitary precaution by an actual doctor. The beak contains herbs that filter the air and cover the horrible stench of the victims of the plague, which is common in this city. I like it because it hides the foul smell of many of the carnival attendees. I will wear the mask with a long black coat, white gloves, and a staff to complete the costume."

They donned their costumes and masks and walked towards the Rialto Bridge. The sun had not yet set, but they were already dodging figures with *papier mâché* masks adorned with fake jewels and feathers. There were children everywhere making trouble and emptying sacks of flour onto each other, as revelers walked in and out of drinking houses and private *palazzi*. On the canal, dozens of gondolas, flat-bottomed *sandolos*, and other vessels full of masked and costumed people sailed by, many of their occupants already drunk.

"What do we do now?" asked Katcher, bewildered.

"First, we find ourselves a café where we can get a meal and our first drinks. Then we start walking the streets. We will soon find impromptu parties on the streets and piazzas and more formal masked balls in private homes, to all of which we will invite ourselves. Bring a purse with coins to give away, but hide it well inside your cloak. This town is always full of pickpockets."

3

For the next few days, Ernst and Friedrich lived through an unbroken succession of masked balls, parades, regattas, and public and private parties. Their activities included vast amounts of drinking and dalliances with women of all ages and conditions. They were continuously amazed by the licentiousness of Venice's women, who sometimes would cast their costumes aside to display their bare breasts out of the windows of *palazzi* to entice visitors.

They pleasantly lost track of time until one afternoon, while the pair were having a very late breakfast of strong Venetian coffee at the Caffé Florian, Friedrich remarked with alarm. "Today is *martedì grasso*, the last day of *Carnevale*. Tomorrow is Ash Wednesday, and this town will close down."

"What do you mean?"

"You might as well be back in Eisenach. Venice in late February is cold and dreary. No more parties, no more easy women or even cross-dressing *gnagas*. Tonight will be our last chance to enjoy the wickedness of this city. Let's get going!"

"Truth be told, I am growing a little weary of all the partying, Freddy. Still, I'm good for one more wild night. *Vesti la baùta*, as some would say."

* * *

Their progress through the streets and piazzas of the old city was slowed by encounters with partygoers they had met in previous days. By now, *I Tedeschi*, as the pair was commonly called, were a well-known sight among those enjoying the *Carnavale*.

They finally arrived, as night fell, to one of their favorite spots, the boat landing in front of the Ca d'Oro palazzo, a short distance north of the Rialto Bridge. There was a large street party in progress and they started their usual routine buying drinks for whoever they engaged in conversation. At some point, Friederich got entangled in an animated dialog with a pretty brunette in maid's costume. Soon they disappeared into the shadows, leaving Ernst looking absently at the waters of the canal.

He was shaken out of his stupor by the arrival of an elegant *pupparin*, a fancy boat traditionally used as a *barca da casada*, or family boat, by the wealthy families of the city. It was being propelled speedily by a pair of oarsmen and carried two passengers sitting on wide benches at the stern of the vessel.

The woman was clearly quite wealthy. She was a strawberry blonde, with a mass of hair set in a complex pouf that utilized wire, cloth, gauze, and other materials to create a voluminous but exquisite coiffure. She was wearing an overflowing red gown and a jewel-encrusted velvet *moretta* mask that was held in place by a button in the mouth that prevented her from speaking. The bodice of the dress hung so low that her nipples showed, covered only by an opulent necklace of diamonds and pearls that protruded from her chest. She was wearing matching diamond and pearl earrings and a ring holding an almost black ruby the size of a quail's egg. In the light of a myriad candles set onboard, she sparkled like a living flame.

By contrast, sitting next to her was a man of indeterminate age dressed in a modest *arlecchino* costume. He wore a half-mask with a short nose and wide, arching eyebrows, and was dressed in rags full of multicolored patches. Though supposedly a servant in the *Commedia dell' Arte* tradition, he appeared more like a bodyguard or a pimp for the woman he accompanied.

The *pupparin* came to a stop right by the landing where Katcher stood. The woman lifted the mask so she could speak: her face was a fascinating mixture of innocence and malice, the delicate beauty of a Botticelli Venus and the hardened, calculating stare of a Carpaccio whore. In a rich alto voice, she greeted him. "*Buona sera, signor Katcher.*"

Surprise at the mention of his name shook Ernst to instant awareness. "Good evening, madame. How do you know my name?"

The woman issued a laugh that was melodious but devoid of warmth. "I make it my business to learn all that happens in *La Serenissima*. You and your companion have become well known during this *Carnevale*."

"What do you know about me?"

"Nothing bad. *I Tedeschi* have built a reputation for generosity and good humor that sits well with the memories set by other Germans who have come to our feast over the years. It is because of your fame that I have come seeking you."

"You honor me, my lady…"

"Please call me Giulietta. And I am no lady. I am a priestess of Venus, and it is my business to bestow enjoyment upon those who seek my services."

Ernst was taken aback by Giulietta's frankness. Recalling his near-death experience on account of his dealings with another prostitute, he responded carefully. "Yours is a noble calling indeed. Yet, I have suffered on account of a previous dalliance with another lady of pleasure…"

"Oh, yes, Gabrielle. She is very skilled."

"Do you know her?"

"*Mon cher*, we are a closely knit circle. I am in touch with every high-class courtesan from London to Warsaw. I rule Venice, as Gabrielle owns Paris. She told me about your eventful encounter with her last year."

"I see. Then you may understand my reluctance to jump into your arms."

"And yet I am prepared to make you a once in a lifetime proposal."

"That's another thing. The money I brought with me from Eisenach is almost exhausted. I am afraid I could not afford the favors of even the lowliest street walker."

Giulietta laughed again; this time her laughter was tinged with irony. "You could not afford my fee with all the money you own. But do not fear. I trade in intangibles."

"What do you mean, intangibles?"

"Things whose value is not measured in coins. You *Tedeschi* are often willing to pay me with intangibles. For example, one of your countrymen, Peter Schlemihl, traded his shadow for the opportunity of spending one night in my arms. More recently, Erasmus Spikher gave up his reflection so that I would grant him one night of pleasure during *Carnevale*. Those goods have no monetary value yet they are appreciated by my master, who finds much use for them." She nodded towards her companion.

Katcher became a bit concerned. "*Signora*, I am a Christian. I believe the Lord has granted us mortal bodies that will one final day be resurrected and saved or damned for all eternity, in their entirety. I could not trade my shadow or my reflection or my immortal soul for a few hours of pleasure, no matter how sublime."

"My dear Katcher, what I am going to ask for is rather trivial, much less important than your shadow. It is something that leaves you with each use, but whose absence will hardly be noticed by others. I will spend this last night of *Carnevale* with you in exchange for your smile."

"My smile? How could that be of value to anyone else?"

The man in Harlequin costume spoke for the first time, in a wheedling tone that Katcher found annoying: "My dear sir, your smile is a manifestation of your joy. I have discovered a way to spread joy among the unhappy by injecting into their spirit the smiles of others more fortunate than them. For me, it is an act of charity that I perform gladly, for what is more generous than meting out the joy that this world needs?"

"Plus," added Giulietta, "there is no loss to you. You give one smile to me today and tomorrow you can give another to someone else, although your joy may be gone."

Ernst remained unconvinced. "This is either a fantasy or a lie. Why would you give me the pleasure of your company in exchange for a smile of joy? What is in it for you?"

"The details of my transaction with Doctor Dapertutto here are of no concern to you. Suffice it to say that in the deal I propose, everyone ends up satisfied."

Ernst felt he had enough of this strange conversation and turned his back on the *pupparin* to go in search of Friedrich. Giulietta spoke again. "I'll give you a free sample."

"What do you mean?"

"Come aboard, sit with me, and I will give you a kiss that will make you want to accept my deal."

Fearing possible foul play, Ernst shook his head and started to leave. Giulietta, moving with surprising speed, got up and, assisted by Dapertutto and the oarsmen, descended onto the landing and stood by the astonished man. "Come, my dear, kiss me. What harm could there be in that?"

Ernst was more than half drunk and felt attracted to the mysterious woman. Turning to Giulietta, he asked dubiously, "Here in the street? In front of the Ca d'Oro?"

"Nobody is watching," she replied, "and we are only hours away from the start of Lent. Who is going to find fault?" Without more, she turned Ernst around, seized him by the waist, and reached up—he was over a full head taller than she—seeking his lips.

He obliged. Holding her by the shoulders, he bent his head and sought shelter in her luscious mouth.

For all he knew, their kiss may have lasted a few moments, or half a day, or an eternity. He lost himself in an ocean of pleasure, a joyous embrace that encompassed the whole universe and left him at the same time sated and desperately in need of more. When their mouths finally separated, he let out a long-contained breath and smiled broadly.

"See? You kissed me, you smiled, and you can do it again."

"So, what is the deal?"

"You sign your name to this paper, promising to give me your smile of joy in perpetuity in exchange for the services I will render, and then we retire to my room and you kiss me again, as many times as you wish, from now until dawn."

"Is that all? And I will wake up safe and sound in the morning?"

"What do you take me for? Do I look like a brigand? You will wake up after the best night of your life, though you probably will not have slept much."

"I still don't understand this deal, but I'm ready to have a good time. Lead the way."

Arm in arm, Giulietta guided Ernst Katcher into the night, Dapertutto following discreetly a few paces behind.

4

Ernst woke up with a start as the morning sun's rays bounced off the nearby lagoon waters. *I have to get up!* was his first thought. He was on the front steps of some *palazzo*, crouched against the front door. He rose painfully, trying to unlock his muscles. He was achy from the exertions of the previous night, but the fear of being arrested as a vagrant blotted out all other concerns, and he took off walking as fast as his stiff legs would carry him.

After a few minutes of aimless wandering, he came to realize where he was: the square known to the locals as Campo San Beneto, not far from his guest house. He made a couple of turns and reached the entrance to his home away from home as Friedrich was coming out, an anxious look on his face.

"Where have you been?" asked his friend as they almost ran into each other. "You were not in our room when I returned last night, and still were not there when I woke up!"

"I was... away," replied Ernst, not knowing how to respond.

"I hope you had a good time," smirked Friedrich.

For the first time since waking up, Ernst searched through his memories. He only had a vague recollection of doing something very pleasant that, however, left a bitter taste in his mind. Indeed, he felt gloomy and increasingly despondent. "I guess so," he muttered.

Friedreich's smile broadened. "It's fine if you won't tell me. We all have our little secrets."

Those words elicited in Ernst the realization that he, indeed, was carrying a secret, one that he dared not reveal even to his closest friend. He sighed and said nothing.

"Well, let's settle our house bill and take off before we get caught in the coming and going traffic," added Friedrich. "You will have plenty of time to let the cat out of the bag, if you wish, during our trip back home."

But Ernst, as he came to remember little by little his encounter with Giulietta, could not bring himself to part with his secret. He felt hopeless and dispirited, increasingly saddened at the realization that all happiness might have slipped away from him, never to return. As the day went on, he became at times snappish or morose, grunting or giving one word replies to Friedrich's attempts at making conversation and refusing to explain the reason for his moodiness. Friedrich eventually gave up and their trip proceeded in uncomfortable silence.

By the time they reached Eisenach, Friedrich no longer treated Ernst Katcher as a friend.

5

As time went by, many others deserted Ernst the way Friedrich had. Fellow noblemen, trades people, servants, the workers in his perfume factory, customers: all who came in personal contact with him were put off by Katcher's disagreeable personality, a state of affairs that he was unable to overcome. His business began to flounder, and he became increasingly isolated.

It was not as if he failed to notice the changes in his personality. To the contrary, he was aware that happiness had been stolen for him, and wondered whether he should look for Dapertutto or Giulietta and try to buy back his joy. Yet such a search might not yield good results; he now realized that they were demonic creatures of some sort and expected that the ransom they would demand for his smile would result in eternal damnation for his soul, a price he was unwilling to pay.

6

Early in December, Ernst decided he needed to make a quick trip to München to discuss with one of his suppliers the delays that were being experienced in the shipping of ingredients for his perfume making operations. After a day of contentious meetings, he left alone to have an early dinner at the Hofbrauhaus, a city landmark he had visited many times in the past.

He was sitting silently in a corner of the large tavern, nursing a tankard of the local beer and reflecting how his mood clashed with the joviality found in places such as this, when he felt a tap on his shoulder and heard a familiar voice.

"Ho, Eri, what are you doing here?"

Katcher's heart skipped a beat. Here was Friedrich, big as life, a man he had not seen in almost a year. How he missed his friend!

He felt guilt and a pang of pain. Trying to keep his emotions in check, he replied in as welcoming a voice as he could muster, "Oh, Freddy! Good to see you!"

Friedrich sat next to Ernst and ordered a beer. While waiting for the serving girl to bring the beverage, Friedrich stared hard at his once best friend, who had withdrawn into silence. "Say, Eri, we need to come clean with each other. What have I done to offend you? Why the long face when you see me?"

Ernst could not keep silent any longer. On the verge of tears, he replied, "No, Freddy, no. I'm not mad at you; there is nothing you have done. It is just that, since Venice, I have lost my spirit, and I'm always in a foul mood!"

The beginning of understanding lit Friedrich's face. "Did something happen in Venice? I had managed to get you in high spirits throughout our stay... except for the day when we got out of town..."

Ernst nodded, still silent.

"You were gone all night just before we left town. Did something bad happen to you then?"

Ernst did not respond.

"Come on, tell me. Did you commit a crime or did something awful? Did you lie with one of those filthy cross-dressing *gnagas*?"

At the end, Ernst could not keep his secret any longer, and in a halting voice told the story of his meeting with Giulietta and the bargain he had struck with the whore. Some parts of the story he could not recall clearly, but the bargain and the ineffable kiss that sealed it were as vivid as if they had occurred an hour before. "See, I'm damned," he concluded, disconsolate.

Friedrich then asked, "Are you sure you are no longer able to experience any joy?"

"I don't think so. I have been despondent since the last time we met, and nothing that I see or hear gets me in a better mood."

"We may be able to put that to the test. An Italian company is in town to perform during our carnival, the *Fasching*, and is doing shows every night at the opera house at Salvatorplatz. They do the types of comic routines we saw in Venice during the carnival. It is vulgar stuff only fit for the masses, but it should be good for a laugh or two. Do you want to come with me? If we hurry, we should be able to catch most of tonight's performance."

Ernst shrugged his shoulders. "Sure, I'll go, but I fear it will be a waste of time."

"We'll see," replied Friedrich, getting his coat on.

7

Although the theater at the Salvatorplatz was new, it was already becoming too small for the needs of the city. The place was packed with patrons, who laughed or shouted their approval of the slapstick performances going onstage. Ernst and Friedrich sat down and proceeded to watch in silence a series of short skits involving pratfalls, actors hitting each other with various objects, prattle in true and imagined languages. The audience hollered and guffawed.

Then, two actors went onstage wearing the garments of low-class servants, calling themselves Arlecchino and Pedrolino. They started having an argument in barbaric German dashed with Italian and French-sounding nonsensical words. While the reasons for the dispute were unclear, the men were fully armed with wooden swords, knives, and pikes, and seemed ready to go at each other.

Their dispute was interrupted by the entrance of a burly man wearing the black cape and tight-fitting uniform of a Spanish soldier. He identified himself as Il Capitano and ordered the servants in a commanding voice to cease their argument. Arlecchino and Pedrolino did nothing of the sort, but continued to heap abuse on each other. Il Capitano sought to separate them, and then both servants turned on Il Capitano and pounded on him with their wooden swords.

The audience broke into raucous laughter, for the fierce-looking soldier cowered as a frightened girl and begged his tormentors to stop. At one point, however, Il Capitano wrestled one of the swords from the combatants and started pummeling Arlecchino vigorously, to the servant's loud outcries and protestations. Something strange happened then: Il Capitano's attacks became fiercer, and his blows started drawing blood. Arlecchino's pleas for mercy rose in intensity as the comedian tried in vain to protect his face and limbs from the savage blows.

Other actors came onstage. Some tried to restrain Il Capitano, while others carried Arlecchino away. An astonished silence enveloped the hall, only to be broken by a single peal of laughter from the stands: Ernst had begun laughing un-controllably.

Friedrich turned to his friend. "You are laughing!" he declared in amazement.

Ernst was now laughing almost hysterically, releasing the pent-up emotions that had held him hostage for many months. He seemed to be going at it so forcefully that his entire body was convulsing, so Friedrich became a little concerned. "Enough, Eri, *basta*! Why are you screaming like this? What happened on the stage was only a *lasso*, a skit. And not a funny one at all!"

With some effort, Ernst Katcher calmed down. When speech returned to him, he explained, "I wasn't laughing at that stupid farce. That whore Giulietta mentioned how her other victims had given up their shadow or their reflection and could only get them back at the cost of their souls. I thought it was going to happen to me also, for losing all prospects of joy in my life seemed unbearable.

"But then I saw this actor, who in my mind stood for Dapertutto, being severely punished, and realized that, even if your joy has been taken away, you can still laugh. Other emotions can prompt laughter; for example, the satisfaction of taking revenge on your enemies."

"That may be true," replied Friedrich. "But it is unbecoming of a Christian, and a gentleman to boot, to take pleasure in avenging himself on his enemies."

Ernst offered no response to Friedrich's remonstration. He knew, in his heart, that his friend was right, but one avenue to recovery from the loss of his joy had been revealed, and he felt secretly satisfied.

Ernst went on laughing, even though the stage action was now an insipid romance.

8

It was the week before Christmas and Eisenach, usually a placid town, was ebullient with activity, as it celebrated the holiday season with its traditional Christmas Market in the city's main square and the courtyard of the Wartburg Castle. Ernst was in no mood for celebration, as was the case most of the time since his ill-fated holiday in Venice the previous year. Thus, he limped through the festivities, ignoring the array of traditional craft shops, strolling musicians, storytellers, vendors of baked goods and hot foods, and providers of mulled wine and brandy to ward against the cold.

For it was biting cold that week. Although warmly dressed and used to the cold, Ernst was shivering as he rushed to his offices near the center of town. When he reached the Marketplatz, which was relatively deserted because of the inclement weather, Ernst stopped to catch his breath and was intrigued by an unexpected sight.

Sitting on the frozen ground, leaning against one of the buildings that circled the square, was a tiny girl dressed in rags, holding a bucket in which passersby had dropped coins and items of food. The girl had a dark complexion and was foreign, Gypsy perhaps, and was shivering from the cold and maybe from some ingrained hunger, for she was thin and privation showed in every muscle of her drawn face.

All the same, while shivering, the girl was tearing small pieces off a loaf of bread she held in one hand and tossing them at a few birds that had gathered around her. She was sharing her meager supper with other beings, just as unfortunate.

Ernst's first impulse was to move on, but the strange scene was compelling. He approached the girl and dropped a coin in her bucket. As he did, he caught a momentary glimpse of happiness in her face, and his own opened into a smile, realizing he had brought joy into someone else's life.

* * *

That night he sent a note to his friend Friedrich in München.

Dear Freddy:

Today I learned that a smile is not like a person's shadow, that can be removed once and for all. Instead, it is like the flowers in the field. There are many types of flowers and many sources of laughter. Some may be gone altogether, but others will return next season unless prevented. I have been preventing all expressions of satisfaction from harboring in my soul. No more. I can still get pleasure from the world without enjoying what it has to offer, and can smile without rejoicing in another's sorrow. My life has been constrained by fate, but I can still live within my bounds and be content, if not happy.

ABOUT THE AUTHOR

Born in Cuba, Matias Travieso-Diaz migrated to the United States as a young man. He is a former engineer and attorney who, following retirement, redirected his efforts towards fiction writing. He lives with his daughter and two dogs in the Washington, D.C. area. He describes himself as an "Animal Farm's goat, Packers and Barça fan, and lover of opera, classical theater, jazz, Italian food, and vino."

He is the author of numerous short stories, over one hundred and seventy of which have been published or accepted for publication in anthologies, magazines, blogs, audiobooks, and podcasts. The first collection of his short stories, *The Satchel and Other Terrors*, was published in 2023 and is available through Dark Owl Publishing. He's also written a novel, *The Taíno Women*, set in Cuba's early colonial period, and a novella, *Lázaro Serrano*, set in Havana in 1762.

Don't miss Matias's first collection of horror short stories...

"Author Matias Travieso-Diaz takes the reader on an engrossing tour of the darkest corners of this world and others, the past, present, dark futures, and even other planes of conscience and reality."
~ Jason J. McCuiston, author of *Project Notebook*

Now available from
Dark Owl Publishing
www.darkowlpublishing.com

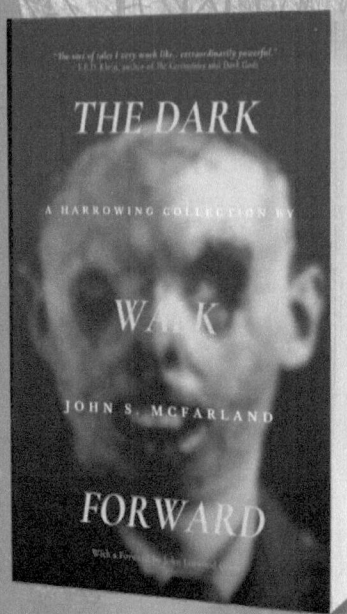